Crystal's smile was visible by the street light filtering through the curtained window as Wilma tucked the support behind her head and shoulders. "Can't lay flat comfortably," she admitted.

Lava spread through Wilma's limbs. Her breasts had a mind of their own, and Wilma guided Crystal's hand to them. All that Wilma had brought into this bed with her was falling away like dead petals from a once fresh flower, leaving her able to bloom again, a different color this time, a different shape, a different blossom.

THE
EROTIC
NAIAD

Love Stories by Naiad Press Authors

Edited by
KATHERINE V. FORREST
and BARBARA GRIER

THE

EROTIC NAIAD

Love Stories by Naiad Press Authors

Edited by
KATHERINE V. FORREST
and **BARBARA GRIER**

The Naiad Press, Inc.
2000

Printed in the United States of America on acid-free paper
First Edition
First Printing November, 1992
Second Printing January, 1993
Third Printing August, 1993
Fourth Printing September 1994
Fifth Printing August, 1995
Sixth Printing January, 1997
Seventh Printing April, 1998
Eighth Printing October, 2000

Cover design by Bonnie Liss (Phoenix Graphics)
Typeset by Sandi Stancil

Library of Congress Cataloging-in-Publication Data

The Erotic Naiad: love stories by Naiad Press authors / edited by Katherine V. Forrest & Barbara Grier.
   p.   cm.
   ISBN 1-56280-026-4
   1. Lesbians—Fiction. 2. Lesbians' writings, American.
3. Erotic stories, American. 4. Love stories, American.
I. Forrest, Katherine V., 1939—   . II. Grier, Barbara, 1933—.
PS648.L47E76   1992
813¢.01083538—dc20
                                         92-18635
                                            CIP

ABOUT THE EDITORS

Katherine V. Forrest

Author of the novels *Curious Wine* (1983); *Daughters of a Coral Dawn* (1984); *Amateur City* (1984); *An Emergence of Green* (1986); *Murder at the Nightwood Bar* (1987), which has been optioned by film director Tim Hunter; a short story collection, *Dreams and Swords* (1987); *The Beverly Malibu* (1989) (Lambda Literary Award winner); *Murder by Tradition* (1991) (Lambda Literary Award winner); and *Flashpoint* (1994).

Articles and book reviews have appeared in a number of publications, including *The New York Times* and *The Los Angeles Times*. All book-length fiction has been published by The Naiad Press, Inc., Tallahassee, Florida. She is co-editor, with Barbara Grier, of *The Erotic Naiad* (1992), *The Romantic Naiad* (1993), and *The Mysterious Naiad* (1994).

Fiction editor, Naiad Press.

Member, PEN International.

Jurist, Southern California PEN fiction award.

Katherine V. Forrest was born in Canada. She has held management positions in business, and since 1979 has been a full-time writer and editor. She lives in San Francisco.

Barbara Grier

Author, editor, bibliographer; writings include *The Lesbian in Literature, Lesbiana, The Lesbian's Home*

Journal, Lavender Herring, and *Lesbian Lives,* as well as contributions to various anthologies, *The Lesbian Path* (Cruikshank) and *The Coming Out Stories* (Stanley and Wolfe). She is coeditor, with Katherine V. Forrest, of *The Erotic Naiad* (1992), *The Romantic Naiad* (1993), *The Mysterious Naiad* (1994). She coedited *The First Time Ever* (1995), *Dancing in the Dark,* (1996) *Lady Be Good* (1997) and *The Touch of Your Hand* (1998) with Christine Cassidy.

Her early career included working for sixteen years with the pioneer lesbian magazine *The Ladder.* For the last twenty-seven years she has been, together with Donna J. McBride, the guiding force behind THE NAIAD PRESS.

Articles about Barbara's and Donna's life are too numerous to list, but a good early overview can be found in *Heartwoman* by Sandy Boucher (New York: Harper, 1982).

She lives in Tallahassee, Florida.

TABLE OF CONTENTS

THE
EROTIC NAIAD
Love Stories by Naiad Press Authors

Edited by
KATHERINE V. FORREST
and **BARBARA GRIER**

Getting to Yes

Nikki Baker

Thalia Bancroft put her hands to her cheeks, both palms feeling red hot, grinning wide and stupid before she could stop herself. She had to turn her head to keep from watching Ann Williams. Looking at Thalia, Adam Brockman, the mayor's aide, thought he must finally be making time. Brockman winked. He was stretched out in his chair with his arms up behind his head like he was on vacation.

School superintendent Dick Dixon was saying, "Blah blah blah blah" to Dave Wideman, the president of the teacher's local, who'd stopped listening. But Ann Williams was laughing at Thalia through the little wrinkles around her eyes. Ann had a slow-breathing sexuality that pulled Thalia in like an undertow.

Thalia fanned her cleavage with the meeting agenda, feeling as though she were going through the change fifteen years too early. Then, she folded her hands across her knees and became the assistant superintendent of schools, her business self. And Dick went on saying whatever he had been saying, his rhetoric just bouncing off Dave Wideman's face like a man playing catch with himself against a brick wall.

There was a strike on. It had gone on long enough that mortgage payments were slipping and teachers with children were drawing on the small fund the union kept for emergencies. It had all come down to people sitting fractured in two lines around a conference table avoiding the ends. And the air was electric, like a walk across a wool rug in the wintertime, static looking for something to spark against.

It appeared the city would have to extend the school year into the summer vacation. That was the kind of shit that lost elections which was why a high level aide like Brockman was here carrying the mayor's ax to grind about the strike timing. This was an election year. So, Dixon kept talking, throwing pitches to Wideman and trying to keep his job and Thalia's, but all she could think about was Ann's brown eyes.

"I'm sure we can all work this out," Dixon was saying.

Thalia watched Brockman crease up his forehead the way he was always warning her about, saying it would wrinkle her face and spoil her looks. Ann's forehead was seamless like a good piece of dark wood furniture somebody cared about. She would age well.

Ann ran her fingers over the tight kinked hair at the crown of her head and down to the nape of her neck where she'd shaved it close. The outline of her breasts broke the line of her good silk dress.

"Blah. Blah, blah, blah," said Adam Brockman.

Dave Wideman sighed through his nose.

And Thalia remembered Ann's dress almost as well as she remembered Ann. The ends of her nails traced the grain of the tabletop and she remembered Ann's fingertips as she withdrew her hand from Thalia's the first time they met, that same simple dress and her big, pretty legs in the low heels, holding out the napkin on which she'd written her number at Thalia's request. The dress was a fine drape of silk and if Thalia knew anything she knew fabric. Her mother had taught her to sew on an old commercial sewing machine that had made all of her clothes until she was halfway through junior high school, a middle-class frugality that she had hated. Thalia looked at the finish of her suit sleeve and smiled. Now she had all of her business clothes made special by a seamstress on the South Side; after her mother's training, she couldn't bear the haphazard workmanship of department stores.

"What goes around, comes around," she said, and was surprised to hear her own voice.

"I beg your pardon, Miss Bancroft. Did you have something you wanted to add to this discussion?" Dave Wideman had a choir boy's voice that sounded like it ought to come from someone else. A huge, red-faced man, his hair was receding from both his forehead and his neck, looking like an Olympic garland.

Ann smiled with the edges of her mouth, so slightly that only Thalia saw. Thalia held onto the smile and let it warm her like an unexpected gift. Ann's eyes ran down her body now like two slow hands on her breasts and belly and Thalia blushed hot again behind her brown skin. "I was just talking to myself."

Wideman rolled his head, once up, once down, as if conferring dispensation.

"Were we talking about the number of teacher's aides?" Adam Brockman yawned.

"Yes we were," said Ann. Her smile was gone and Thalia thought for a moment she had just imagined it. Ann was an elementary school teacher and what people here, teachers included, didn't seem to understand was that she had her thirty kids eight hours every day and she needed an aide to even get her planning done. The last budget cut had taken away her part-time aide and she was making do with volunteer moms. She'd dialed her way through this year's class list with no success. Women who didn't have to work didn't send their kids to public schools and she didn't have a minute in her day to breathe, let alone put her lesson plans together.

Ann was just waiting for Dave Wideman to try to give away her aides in exchange for something she couldn't use. She sighed. But God, wasn't Thalia looking better every time she saw her. Ann put away her consideration of Thalia Bancroft's breasts and set her jaw for a street fight.

"So what about the teacher's aides?" Wideman said. "If you'll think about our spousal benefits package, I think we can be flexible about these aides."

Ann's face seized up. "I told you, Dave. I need my aide at least three days a week." She whispered to Wideman: "We talked about this and we agreed."

"There's an aide in the city's proposal," Thalia said. "I think you'll be very pleased if you just consider the package as a whole."

"I've read the proposal." Ann's voice was so sharp it cut Thalia around the edges. "The aide is two days a week, half-time. I've got thirty kids and I can't be spending my time standing around at lunch unscrewing thermos tops. Not if the mayor wants these kids to learn to read."

"We'll talk about it later." Wideman's voice sounded choked.

"We'd better talk about it now," Ann said.

Wideman pressed his lips together and then opened them again. "All right," Wideman said. "The aide is half-time and there are no benefits."

Dixon cleared his throat. "Of course there are benefits." The room was hot and the overhead lights caught the sweat on his face shining at the edges of his kinky hair. Dixon paged through his proposal. "They're very clearly outlined here." He smiled when he found his page and read the passage out. "I think we've been very generous. Besides —" Dixon shrugged mildly. "It's all we can do."

"You can't have more slices than you've got pie, eh?" Brockman said.

Wideman crossed his arms. He sat back in his chair with his legs wide open and his suit bunched up in the crotch. "I was speaking figuratively," Wideman said. "Figuratively speaking, there might as well be no benefits, Richard." He worked his knees in and out. "The mayor's staff has benefits, or so I hear."

"It's the best we can do," Brockman said. He'd grown red underneath his golf tan. "It's fair."

Wideman swiveled his chair from side to side with the balls of his feet. Thalia was watching Ann, but Ann's face was like Wideman's, closed and hard.

"Take it or leave it," Brockman said.

A panic smile ran over Richard Dixon's face, spread out like warm butter at a picnic. "I don't think that's what the mayor's office means," he said. "Now, this deal is fair. But, hell, there's nothing written in stone around here, Dave. What Adam means is put something of your own out on the table."

"Take it or leave it," Brockman said. "That's what we mean."

Thalia dropped her head and shaded her eyes with her hand. She watched Wideman lean across the table and put himself in Brockman's face.

"If that's the mayor's deal, you tell him I think we'll leave it."

Wideman marched his people out behind him like the tribes of Israel.

Ann's dress flapped at the backs of her knees. Thalia watched her go with a sudden despair and she let her breath out in a closed-mouth sigh.

"They'll be back," Brockman muttered.

Dixon didn't smile and the teachers delegation didn't come back that day. At 6:30 p.m. Brockman looked at his watch and asked Thalia out to dinner.

"It doesn't have to be business," Brockman said when she declined. He ran his hand over his thin blond hair and checked his look in the windows of the hotel.

"Maybe next time." Thalia liked Brockman for his resilience. You needed that in a city appointment — that and shamelessness.

Brockman slid into the back of the Checker cab and held the door open for her. "Can I drop you anywhere?" He never gave up. But Thalia had her car.

Thalia took the long way home, four miles north past where she was going, to Ann Williams' neighborhood, wondering if she could remember the address. She had met Ann at a fund-raiser eighteen months ago, for a black circuit court candidate. Ann had been single and looking, a friend of a friend and Thalia had been interested but very married. Not so married that Ann's handshake hadn't thrilled her. Thalia hadn't had a date since her lover, Amy, left. She wondered if she and Ann might have more in common, the negotiation notwithstanding. Her stomach pitched and she thought that at least from her end they had chemistry.

Ann opened the door up wide as if Thalia's visit pleased her and she cinched up the belt of her terrycloth robe in the breeze. "Won't you come in off the stoop, Miss Bancroft." She winked. "I wouldn't want the teacher's union to think I was consorting with the enemy."

Thalia stood in the entryway. "Have you talked to Elaine lately?" She closed the door behind her. Elaine had introduced them; it was all she could think to say and she wondered if Ann could hear her heart beating or knew how her face was warming under Ann's smile.

"Did you come all the way up here to ask me that?" Ann took her jacket easily and hung it on a wooden hook by the door. "Or were you going to interrogate me about the teacher's contract strategy? It won't get you anywhere but come on in anyway, baby. I don't want you to go telling Elaine I was rude."

Ann smiled and walked Thalia towards her little galley kitchen. "If you want a drink, you're welcome," she said. "I was having one myself." Ann poured another glass of jug wine from the refrigerator and set it on the counter by the stove. Water was running in the sink. "You don't mind if I do my dishes?" she asked. "I wasn't expecting anybody."

Ann bent over the sink. She was happy for the company. Her garden apartment seemed smaller and darker when she was alone. Thalia filled it up the way furniture can make a room look bigger.

Thalia leaned against the counter drinking her wine and watching Ann. "I read this book called *Getting to Yes*," Thalia said. "It's about negotiating."

"I thought we weren't going to talk business."

Ann wiped her soapy hands on the pockets of her
robe.

"This is just ideas." Thalia sipped her wine. Ann's
voice made her giddy and she was looking for her
balance again. "The negotiation didn't go the way
anybody wanted," Thalia started. "I thought you and
I could talk about it and then maybe work
something out to put on the table tomorrow. What
can ideas hurt?"

"You know —" Ann shook her head. "You're not
even supposed to be here tonight." She put a dish in
the sink to drain and pulled the next one out of the
water. Thalia was proving a disappointment. A year
and a half ago, Ann had given out her number only
to find that Thalia was tied up with some other
woman long-term, found out by calling her up and
getting her lover on the phone. Then, Thalia had
hemmed and hawed about how she'd only meant to
network. Now here she was, come around to talk
about negotiating like she was doing Ann a favor,
without word one about how she'd wanted to call but
couldn't and wasn't it lucky that she was single
again.

"The first thing is to separate people from the
problems. Like tonight I'm not the administration,"
Thalia was saying, "I'm Thalia Bancroft, not the
enemy, all right?" Thalia stood behind Ann at the
sink and rubbed her shoulders. "Relax. The next
thing is to think about the things we have in
common."

Ann hung a dishtowel over her shoulder and sat
a hand on her hip and laughed. "Do you mean you
don't want me to have to work all summer either? Is
that it, baby?" Ann used the word baby like a deep,

slow kiss and knew its effect and laughed again. "Is that what you're talking about?"

"Well, like that." Thalia let her breasts brush against Ann's back. Her nipples stiffened under the thin silk of her blouse. "And like, I like you and maybe you like me." She slid her hands down to Ann's hips. She pressed her lips against the short hair on the back of Ann's neck and whispered, "What would you say to a part-time aide, Miss Williams?"

Ann dried her dishes pretending to ignore Thalia's lips on her neck but she felt warm under her robe despite herself. She knew her thighs were wet. "I'd say the city wins all around." Ann was irritable at her own weakness.

"Maybe everybody wins." Thalia stood so close Ann could hear her breathe. She let her hands fight the knot of Ann's robe until the terrycloth fell away from her hips and Ann guided Thalia to the soft curly hair between her legs. Her breath caught short and fast. Thalia imagined the taste of her, the way you can smell water in the dark, saw the place held open and wet in her hands and kissed the short neck hair with her tongue.

Ann smelled of musk and hard soap, and her sighs were soft and rocking. Between their bodies, the robe stroked Ann's lips full and ripe, came away wet on Thalia's thigh. Ann anchored Thalia's cheeks in her hands and when she came, Thalia felt the shudder of her own hips.

Ann turned and kissed her open-mouthed. She worked the buttons of Thalia's blouse and breathed through her mouth with her lips just parted, tasting first. And then more deeply. Ann's tongue was warm and rough against her own, lolled back to the shallows of her teeth like high tide lapping at the cracks of rocky beaches, telling stories that felt like the hot breath of wetted lips on the skin of eyelids.

Ann pulled down the lace of Thalia's underwear. She cupped and rubbed her in her palm, sending heat and aching need up the center of Thalia's body and weakness rolling down to the break of her knees and Ann would not let her come. She kneaded slowly with her fingers and the back of her hand stroked the silk of Thalia's panties.

She worked the hooks of Thalia's bra until it came away with a snap. It lay on the floor like the broken wings of a blackbird and Ann took Thalia's breast in her mouth, first just the tan button of her nipple, run along the edges of her teeth and then her whole breast as if Ann would eat her slowly, swallowing her like a snake. Thalia sighed with the long hiss of steam from a tea kettle. She held Ann's head to her breast, prayed for the success of her hungry moans. She fought Ann's hands with the motion of her hips.

And in the bedroom, they lay side by side. Eyes closed, they breathed the heat of each other's breath and the room was thick with the smells of their satisfaction. It made Thalia too drunk to sleep. Hope, sucked in like opium smoke from a long thin pipe, promised the future with the optimism of cocaine.

Ann kissed her with a mouth that did not rest, pressed down over the length of her body, mouth to mouth, grinding hip to thigh. She worked her way down from Thalia's throat to the paunch that sat below her belly as if she walked a well worn path fondly, stopping for memories. She went with her fingers firmly into the places that Thalia thought she had forgotten. Her body sucked and caught Ann's fingers as they came and went deeper at each return. Their motion smacked softly like a closed-mouth kiss and Ann gasped as if she herself were being penetrated. Thalia heard her own pleasure as if it came from someone else. The sound fed itself on the rhythm of Ann's fingers; it built like a distant train and stopped with a catch of breath and a sigh of completion.

Dave Wideman helped himself to the coffee at the center of the table and swallowed hard. "Let's get to it." He grimaced over his cup.

"All right," Dixon said. Adam Brockman, he explained, could not attend, having pressing meetings today with the mayor. "Where were we?"

"We were talking about teacher's aides," said Thalia.

Ann Williams grinned at her from across the room.

Dixon opened his arms. "All right, Dave," he said. "Talk to me."

Summer Sojourn

Jackie Calhoun

We lay melting on the pier in the hot sun, my head on my arms, my eyes level with her cleavage. I found myself staring, wanting to feel the softness, to separate and define the breasts with a finger, to wipe away droplets of perspiration collecting in the cleft. Lifting my gaze, I met her eyes laughing at me with the knowledge of my desire. A thrill shot through me. Still, I only looked.

When the sun began to set, staining the sky with shades of red, we gathered our belongings and started toward the cottage. The smell of pines and lake brought back memories of other summers, other friends, other times.

After changing into dry clothes, we moved around the small kitchen, occasionally brushing against each other. And every time we did I felt a rush of excitement.

Eating on the porch overlooking the lake, we watched the light fade from the sky. A nearly full moon rode through the heavens accompanied by a few bright stars. June bugs buzzed and battered themselves against the screens. A fragrance, some wild flowering bush, entered the room on a soft, warm breeze.

"Do you realize," Beth said, "that this is the first time we've been alone for more than a few hours?"

"Really?" I felt her hand touch mine and I jerked as if from something hot. "I hadn't thought about it, I guess." Not true. All I had thought about was when and if and how and where this friendship was heading. Or was there even something to go somewhere? Some days I wasn't sure of that.

We had been close friends for months, having met at work. I knew Beth's interest in me was unlike that of my other women friends. There was an intimacy in her glances, in her touch, in her questions and comments. When I asked her to the lake this weekend, I realized I was inviting her advances.

Now she smiled, sweet and knowing and loving, causing my heart to jump into an erratic beat. "Let's do it," she whispered.

"What?" I asked, suddenly unable to draw a deep breath.

"What's wrong with a little lovemaking and I do love you, you know." She raised a golden eyebrow as if to emphasize her words.

"I love you too," I murmured.

She laughed and stood up, grasping my hand and pulling me to my feet. "Come on, Shelley."

The bedroom smelled of the heady night brought in on that same current of air. We stood uncertainly at the foot of the double bed and looked into the shadows of each other's eyes. Her laugh, nervous and throaty, sounded again.

"I feel like a kid," she said.

When it came to women, I was a kid. I'd never done this before. Perhaps that was why I couldn't move and barely breathed.

"It's not so different with a woman, you know," she said. "You start by kissing." And she leaned forward and touched my lips with hers, her tongue grazing mine.

My pulse pounded in my throat, in my ears, in my chest. I stood there trembling, my legs rubbery. Her mouth felt soft and warm as it moved over mine.

She placed her hands on my arms, ran them up to my shoulders and down my chest to my breasts where they gently held my heart. "You're beautiful," she said quietly, "with your dark curling hair and your blue-black eyes and your wonderful breasts."

Did she mean it? I thought I heard a smile in her voice, and I believed she was the beautiful one

— her hair nearly blond from the summer sun, her eyes wide and deeply blue like the lake on a bright day. We stood a breath away and I couldn't speak. When I felt her lips brush mine again, I closed my eyes.

Still holding my breasts, she moved her mouth from the corner of mine to my cheek and eyes and neck.

I shivered.

"Cold?" she whispered in my ear.

I shook my head.

"Take this off," she said and gently tugged at my shirt, pulling it over my head.

I opened my eyes then and tentatively touched her bare arms, feeling skin smooth and warm. Slipping out of my grasp, she slid my shorts and panties down my legs and knelt to press her face against my belly. Tracing her shoulders and following the curve of her neck, I combed my fingers through the thickness of her hair. It fell in silken strands to tickle my skin along with her soft, uneven breathing.

She kissed her way up my body, taking my nipples to suckle, and I felt in my groin the tugging at my breasts. Eager now, I helped her out of her clothes and shyly looked at her nakedness, at her skin glowing in the meager light from the moon and a lamp in the next room.

Her breasts were firm and full and laced with delicate blue veins, the nipples pale. My gaze swept over her, taking in her rib cage narrowing to slight curve of stomach, the button of navel, a flat abdomen widening to slim hips, curly dark-blond wedge of hair under it. I managed a deep, shaky breath.

We lay on the bed and for the first time I felt the soft comfort of breasts against each other. Sighing, I pressed myself to her. And she sought my mouth with hers, exciting me anew with urgent kisses. Lips warm, tongues searching.

Then I felt her hand between my legs — seeking, caressing, penetrating — and I sucked in air. All of me paused, waiting, honing in on the sensation of her touch. An exquisite ache gathered and grew with the rhythm of her gentle stroking, mounting until I moved with it. When I thought I could no longer bear the intensity, she slid warm fingers inside me. But as she slowly withdrew them to resume stroking, the throbbing pleasure set me moving again.

Several times she brought me close to climax and staved it off by entering me — until I hung quivering, suspended by desire while the blood pounded through me toward her touch. When I could sustain the passion no longer, the ache exploded, leaving me weak and panting. Only then did I realize that the throaty noises I had been hearing were my own.

She slipped her fingers back inside me as if to hold in the feeling. And when my breathing became controlled, she gathered me close in her arms and kissed my face softly.

"Did you like that?" she asked.

I laughed, hardly recognizing the sound. I knew I would have to try to please her and briefly feared that I might fail. But the desire just to touch her overwhelmed my anxiety. I tasted her mouth, her tongue, with mine. Then I kissed her throat and breasts and put my hand between her legs in a hesitant touch. Enthralled, I gently worked my fingers into the tangle of hair to the warm wetness within. Sliding my fingers over the silky softness, I tried to remember how I myself felt and slid a finger into her depths. She made another husky sound, similar to the groan I had heard when I first touched her intimately.

I caressed her as she had stroked me, slowly at first, just exploring and listening to her respond with little moans. I felt with wonder the leaves of her clitoris, traced the folds with gentle fingers, slipping first one finger inside, then two — stroking faster, rhythmically. She began to move and I joined her, my legs entwined around one of hers. She panted and my breathing quickened. Her excitement became my own. When she shuddered in release, she took hold of my wrist. I gently pulled free and covered her dampness with my hand as she had done mine.

We slept then, wrapped around each other, the soothing breeze drying the sweat on our skins. I dreamed of nothing and wakened to her touch. Moonlight flooded the room. I felt her warm breath against my back and her hand between my legs. The gentle, insistent search demanded admittance and I opened myself to her. Rolling face down, I felt the exquisite ache begin to surge again, felt her cover me with her body, her breasts against my back, her hips moving with mine.

After, I lay quietly for a few minutes until she turned me over and held me to her. Moving downward to suckle her breasts and bury my face in their softness, I inhaled the smell of her. Winding her legs around me, she began to move against me, and I put my arms over her hips and reached between her thighs to submerse myself in her desire. As she moved, I let my fingers slide with her rhythm. She turned us until she was on top, and I lifted my face to hers to kiss her, to take her tongue in my mouth. The pulse throbbing in her neck matched the pounding of my heart.

When we fell asleep again, the moon had nearly set. We awakened to birds singing, to squirrels chasing through branches, to sunlight and puffy white clouds racing across the sky on a warm wind. I sat up and saw the lake, blue and restless, sunshine glinting off its waves. Suddenly shy in the light of day, I turned and smiled at Beth and was rewarded with a grin.

"Come here," she said, drawing me down next to her.

She blanketed me with her body, then turned, her hips toward my face, and I pulled them to me. Her sex opened like a small red flower and I tasted it. The warm, salty sweetness of her aroused me and I thrust into her, eliciting a moan from both of us. Throbbing pleasure coursed through me, blood thumping toward the flickering of her own tongue on me, and I could only control it by concentrating on her. She moved against me, even though I held her hips firmly. Tracing each other gently with our tongues, we rushed toward climax, each pushing against the other, riding a tide until the waves crashed over and released us.

Holding to her tightly in the aftermath, I felt spent and exultant at the same time — a shipwrecked survivor washed up on the shore of a lovely island.

"How do you like making love with a woman?" Beth asked, a little laugh in her voice, lying on her back with one arm around me.

"I don't like it, I love it," I replied, burrowing into her side, getting as close as I could. With one hand I touched the highlights of her body; the breasts spreading a little, the pale pink tips hardening under my fingertips, the now slightly concave abdomen, the damp curly triangle.

She smiled and turned her head to kiss my nose. "Want to go out and enjoy the day?"

We washed each other in the lake, removing our suits as soon as we entered the cool water. Then, encircled by towels, we dried on the pier. Sitting cross-legged in the sunshine, we shared a breakfast of fresh fruit.

Morning turned into afternoon in a haze of heat. Even the wind blew hot. Radiating contentment, I slept and awakened to swim again. Beth joined me and when we pulled ourselves onto the pier to dry, we lay side by side, face to face. She lifted her eyebrows in question, causing my heart to leap and me to realize that this was the cue I had been waiting for since morning. I smiled and nodded my reply.

As I started to collect our possessions, Beth said, "Leave them for now." She placed a hand on my shoulder and we walked together to the cottage.

Lesbian Cartoons

Rhonda Dicksion

What You Want, Sometimes

Lauren Wright Douglas

What you want, sometimes, is this.

Anonymity. No names, no addresses, no phone numbers. No questions, no answers. No eloquence, no lies.

Just desire's truth. That little and that much.

Tonight, in this dim throbbing place, under the lurid lights, you select her. She is a banker in tweeds, she is a biker in leather, she is a trucker in denims, she is a teacher in linen. She is what you want. You allow her to stalk you, to snare you on the hook of her gaze and reel you in like a trout.

Landed, you leave things to her. Your cigarettes lie on the table between you. With clever fingers she extracts one, holds it to your mouth. You bend to accept it with your lips and the V of your fingers. Light flares. Her hands cup a match. She brings the tiny flame to you, and you accept it, looking up to meet her eyes, knowing that she sees the other conflagration you desire. *Yes,* you tell her without words. *Yes,* she answers.

Now, outside, in the alley, you put your back against the brick wall and wait. There is a streetlight out on the boulevard but here the shadows have gathered.

In your bones and the soles of your feet, you feel a deep, bass thrumming. Is it the club's music or some interior urgency? No matter.

Then she is here. She has come after you as you knew she must. Leaning against the wall, leaning over you, she is another shadow, an incarnate piece of the darkness. You sense that she will now open her mouth to say something and you put a hand over her lips. *No words,* your hand tells her.

She smiles, and you see her teeth gleam feral in the streetlight. You like that. When she pulls you to her, you like that, too. You smell soap and musk, feel the roughness of cloth, hear the rasp of breathing and suddenly even these are too wordy, too intrusive. What you want is something more primal. You take her hands and put them against your flesh, under your shirt, and she runs her palms over your skin, making you gasp, making you writhe, making you wet.

In silence, she unbuttons you. When she bends to you, you feel lips, teeth, tongue, and then a warmth, a molten weight, a nova approaching critical mass just below your belt buckle.

You twist, clamped in the vise of her hands. You ache. To wait any longer is intolerable. You let her know. You want her hand jammed down your jeans, between your legs, her fingers a presence inside you, her lips on your lips, her teeth against yours, her tongue in your mouth. You want to be opened, peeled, spread, devoured. You want to be pierced to the heart. And then you want the huge, hot, supernova which comes roaring down your veins, along your nerves to seize you and hurl you finally into someplace vast and far, into the hush of space where you float, mute and spent, while all around you the world's uttered, unnecessary words stream past like sparks from a summer's bonfire, like a bright rain of comets, flare, then fade to black.

And then she is gone.

Just desire's truth. That little and that much.

And that is what you want, sometimes.

Recipe for a Salad

Jennifer Fulton

Renee was contemplating an array of vegetables when I stuck my head in her window.

"Getting dinner?" I inquired, looking at my watch. It was only four. I'd left work early and was panting for a coffee.

"Not yet," she said and beckoned me in.

I battled my way through the jungle on her doorstep — Renee called it her portable garden — and sprawled into the huge armchair beside her table.

Renee looked over her shoulder at me. She had beautiful shoulders; smooth, strong, with tiny dark freckles sprayed across them. She had the same freckles on her nose, just across the bridge. Every now and then I wanted to grab her and see if I could lick them off. But that's strictly the kind of kinky thing a lover would do and Renee and I were not lovers.

"You want me to peel something?" I offered, eyeing the vegetables.

It was a pretty strange assortment. Zucchini, cucumber, carrots, bananas. Renee was obviously making one of her weird salads. Probably having some vegetarian to dinner and wanting to impress her.

Renee said no. She preferred them with the skins on.

Tonight's woman was a hardliner, I decided. Sunflower seeds between meals, eight glasses of spring water a day, desserts that tasted like peanuts. "So who is it tonight then?" I inquired, extending my legs and folding my arms. Renee looked me up and down with her dark, dark eyes.

"Nosey parker."

I shrugged. Completely shameless. "What's she like?"

Renee just smiled. A secretive kind of smile that made me feel like I'd just been left out of the best joke of the year.

Suddenly I was pissed off at the woman who could make her smile that way. What was so special about her? What did she have that I didn't?

I wasn't jealous, not really. A little piqued,

maybe. Kind of titillated and disappointed at the same time.

Renee was engrossed in the vegetables again and I wondered suddenly if they were art, not a meal at all. They were laid out on her table in neat little rows, from the smallest to the biggest, and Renee was picking each one up and putting it down again with an assessing look.

I said, "I'll make the coffee if you like."

Renee said, "Sure," and held up a pair of those long acid free cucumbers. "What do you think, Dale?"

"Of cucumbers in general or those in particular?"

"Of these. Here, feel them," she offered.

I looked at her strangely. Had my friend finally cracked up? Had her bizarre lifestyle pushed her over the edge at last?

It had to happen, I thought a little smugly. Hadn't I warned her? You can't just stay home and draw pictures all day, refuse to watch television, and practice non-monogamy, without something giving.

I stared at the cucumbers, gave them a cursory squeeze and commented, "Nice and fresh."

Renee smiled her knockout dazzling smile at me, and her nearly black eyes sparkled recklessly. If any other woman had looked at me that way, my stomach would have bounced along the floor and rolled at her feet. But Renee wasn't flirting. We were friends. We'd been friends for three years.

I'd met Renee at a party. She was moving in on a buddy of mine, Lee-ann the truckie. For a tough butch, Lee-ann had crumbled faster than shortbread. One of those dark-eyed sparkles and she'd come over all hot and bothered.

When Renee had had enough of stringing her
along in front of an audience, they'd gone home
together, Lee-ann shrugging helplessly at me.

Their fling lasted about two months and in the
course of it I learned that Renee lived just a few
houses away from me. I ended up having dinner at
her place a couple of times. She was a good cook
and Lee-ann wanted to show her off.

After they'd gone their separate ways — no hard
feelings — I met Renee at her gate one evening and
she invited me in for coffee. Imagining that maybe I
was being lined up to be the new girl in her life, I
was thrilled.

It took six months and a lot of Renee's very fine
coffee before I worked out what was happening.
Renee and I were making friends. For all that she
was a flirt, and went through women like the rest of
us use toothpaste, Renee didn't have many friends.

She found it hard to get close to women, she
confessed after nearly a year. I wondered what she
was going on about, given she'd slept with two that
I knew of just that week. But after a while I
understood that it was her pattern. Renee slept with
women she barely knew, then sent them away before
that could change.

Lee-ann was one of her longest flings, as it
turned out. Two whole months. Migod, they'd almost
got to know each other. Once I'd figured it out, I
was woolly headed with relief. I was not destined to
be one of these candles in the wind. I was Renee's
friend, not some fly-by-night sexual plaything.

Her place became my second home. The two

lovers I had over the subsequent years just had to live with it. Knowing Renee's reputation, neither of them could.

So I became single and celibate. I didn't mind. By thirty a woman isn't ruled by her hormones, is my belief.

"I was thinking about sex," Renee announced.

I snorted. "Well, that's a real change."

She nudged me with a reproachful toe. I sipped my coffee virtuously.

"I mean I've decided to give up on it for a while . . ." she went on.

I choked. "Why?" I met her eyes. She seemed totally serious. "Have you got a disease?"

Renee looked scathing. "Of course not! I'm not that careless. What I mean is I'm giving up on lovers for a while."

I stared at her. I couldn't conceal my astonishment. "What's brought this on?"

She looked so shy for a moment that a nasty suspicion entered my mind. "Have you fallen for someone?" I demanded.

"No . . ." she said, but the hesitation told a whole different story.

Suddenly I wanted to grab her, shake the truth out of her. I put my coffee on the floor, told myself to settle down. My hands were shaking.

"Dale." Renee came over to me, perching on the wide cushioned arm of my chair. She took my hand. "Don't be angry at me," she whispered.

I looked at the floor. I just couldn't bear it when she went all pleading like that. It made me feel like a cruel mother bullying a little child. I felt her fingers in my hand, warm and trusting. If Renee couldn't be honest with me, who else was there?

I got my act together, behaved like a true friend. I pulled her down into my lap and gave her a cuddle. Renee loved to cuddle. She always said she felt so safe with me. And of course she was.

"So you're giving up sex ..." I prompted, making like my therapist.

"I'm giving up lovers," Renee corrected. "And if I want sexual gratification, I'm going to look after myself ..."

"Uh huh," I said, ever the good listener.

"That's how come I'm checking out the vegetables."

I missed her point. "You what?"

"I read about it," Renee told me. "Vegetables are a natural sex toy. I thought it might be better than using those electric things."

I thought about my vibrator. "I doubt it, Renee." The voice of experience. I mean, *vegetables???*

Renee pulled back slightly, sought my eyes. "You think I'm weird?"

"No ... no." I shook my head quickly. "I mean if you want to have a relationship with a vegetable, go ahead. Straight women do it all the time." I sniggered at my own joke, then fell silent.

Her eyes left mine, tears hovering about their corners. "I thought you would understand," she said, moving off my knee.

I pulled her back, forgetting myself for a moment, and held her very close. She smelled like lilies and summer. I leaned my cheek into her thick chestnut hair and murmured, "I'm sorry Renee, I really am. Sometimes I'm just tactless."

She looked at me gravely. "I'm serious about this Dale. I want to try something different."

I glanced across at the vegetables. This was not the time to be jealous of a cucumber. "I think it's a good idea," I said, straight-faced.

Renee shifted on my knee, leaned back against the chair arm and sighed. "I'm sick of sleeping with different women all the time."

"Why?" I ventured. They couldn't all be lousy in bed.

"I feel guilty a lot," said my friend. "Some of them are so nice ... and I know I've hurt women's feelings ..."

I nodded. More than one casualty had arrived on my doorstep demanding to know what I'd said to put Renee off them.

"I just can't seem to stop myself," Renee said. "As soon as I've got them into bed, I'm bored. And if I'm not bored I get scared. And if I like them and I start seeing them, then they think it's a relationship ... so I have to dump them."

I was out of my depth. "Have you considered talking to a therapist?" I ventured.

Renee beamed at me. "I've been going for six months. That's what all this is about. I've realized I have a problem with intimacy."

I tried to look surprised, impressed. I didn't gloat and say I told you so. I reached up and stroked the hair back from her face, letting my fingers slide illicitly into the springy curls. Renee closed her eyes and leaned into my hand.

"You're the only person I can talk to," she said. "The only one I trust."

I should have felt touched, happy in our friendship. Instead I felt trapped.

She inched her way around, nestled against me, head on my shoulder. I draped my arms loosely about her, dropped furtive kisses on her hair.

Renee sighed. "I wish . . ."

"You wish?"

She shrugged, turned her face up to me. Her eyes were dark and appealing, her mouth softly parted. I wanted to make love to her. I took a sharp ragged breath and felt hot color swamping my cheeks.

"I wish too," I said and cupped her face tenderly in one hand, bent to kiss her. My mind screamed at me to stop before I ruined everything. What happened to boundaries? Trust?

Her lips were warm, trembling slightly. I kissed her more firmly, wound my fingers into her hair and pulled her even closer.

Goodbye friendship, chanted the guilt choir in my head. You've really blown it now, kid.

I ignored them, kissed her neck, the freckled shoulders. Her arms clung to me. I hoisted us up out of that chair, caught her to me hard and stood passionately kissing her, there in the kitchen beside the vegetables.

She was kissing me back, murmuring my name, telling me she wanted me. Then we were in her bedroom, undressing each other clumsily, shakily. And she never stopped kissing me till we were naked and touching each other as we'd never touched.

Everything felt so right; the vanilla velvet scent of roses drifting through the window, the late sun flooding the room with hot gold. I tipped Renee onto the cool sheets and lightly, sweetly, kissed her mouth. I covered her with my body; my flesh, my being, caressing hers. Our hearts were beating one against the other, our fingers entwined, our breath merging.

"I'm wetter than rain," she whispered damply on my cheek, and wrapped her legs around me.

She took me inside her the same way she let me into her life; slowly, deliberately, and thrillingly. And I lost myself the way I never had; immersed and wanton, my senses brimming, until there was only her, and time and place and thought were suspended in exquisite oblivion.

Later, as we lay moistly cocooned, she caught my hand quite suddenly in hers and smiled like sunshine after a storm. "I love you Dale," she said.

I smiled back at her. "I love you too, Renee."

The next day we made the most peculiar salad out of those vegetables. Renee called it the Big Discovery Salad. She gives the recipe away without a blink.

Flowers

Penny Hayes

What on earth was she *doing* here? What had possessed her? It wasn't like she was a kid, for God's sake. She was a gray-haired, fifty-five-year-old woman who had no business in the bed of another woman she'd never met before two hours ago. And worse, she was naked — *naked,* her clothes over there on the chair where she couldn't even reach them without surrendering the sheet she held tightly clenched against her chin.

She swallowed hard watching Crystal's sleek body

swaying before the full-length mirror — seductively, Wilma supposed — to some inner rhythm only Crystal could hear.

God, Crystal was beautiful. Thirty-five years ago, Wilma had looked like that, sinewy arms, hips narrow as a boy's, back muscles undulating beneath a deep tan, one chin, not a mark on her flesh anywhere.

Crystal slowly drew a brush through her long black hair. The satiny threads floated crackling and sticking to the bristles until the electricity released them. Ghost-like, they resettled against her shoulders. "You've made love how many times?" she asked. Her brown eyes were bright and smiling.

"Six for sure," Wilma said. "The kids are grown and gone now, but ... six for sure."

Crystal turned from the mirror, her buttocks as round and tight as two freshly picked melons. "You've made love six times for sure because you've borne six children?"

Wilma laughed nervously. "I've made love many more times than that, of course." She didn't want to sound like some old dried-up prune.

Crystal walked over to Wilma and propped a foot on the edge of the bed where Wilma lay. Her legs spread slightly as she rested an arm on her knee.

Wilma tried not to look, tried not to see the black curly hair, the pink bud hidden within. A musky, pleasant odor drifted toward her. Her gaze fell away.

If only she hadn't had that fight with Harold, hadn't screamed at him that sleeping with a woman might be better than thirty-five years of sleeping with him had been, hadn't gone to that woman's bar that she knew about but had never dreamed of going to, she wouldn't be here now.

Crystal sat down beside her, her breasts jutting forward, young, creamy looking, the nipples relaxed. "No, Wilma, you haven't made love before. Ever. But you can now. Right now — and then you can go home knowing you've made love at least once in your life."

Confused, Wilma said, "But I just told you . . ."

Crystal put her finger to Wilma's lips. "I know what you told me." Her finger slid down the creases leading from each side of Wilma's nose to the corners of her mouth. "The lines of many smiles — and of wisdom. They're very attractive."

Wilma eased her grip on the sheet. Her arthritis was driving her nuts tonight. "The lamp," she said. Her eyes slid in the direction of the light.

"I'll dim it." Crystal switched the light to low and lay on her side drawing over her body what sheet remained after Wilma's gluttonish take-over. She propped herself up on an elbow. "Have you ever known a lesbian, Wilma?"

"Never. Read about them in stories, though."

Crystal shifted her weight. "What'd they say?"

It could have been an accident that Crystal's thigh touched Wilma's, but Wilma didn't move. She had come here for a purpose. She was going to punish the hell out of Harold. She shrugged. "The books didn't say much about . . . uh . . . lesbians. They play ball and are pretty big and aggressive."

Crystal fell back, roaring with delight. She tossed aside the covers, her stomach muscles knotting with laughter. Tears rolled down the sides of her cheeks and her even white teeth flashed in the lamp's soft light. "Wilma, you've got to stop reading all that fifties crap. Oh, God, if the old dykes could only hear you."

"I live in a small world," she said defensively.

"You live in your husband's world, Wilma. I'm glad you chose to spend a little time in mine."

Crystal drew near and Wilma studied her face. "You don't have a single age line, do you?"

Crystal smiled broadly. "Not in this light. My skin is much more honest in the telling light of day."

"I should have such skin," Wilma said. If Crystal came any closer, their lips would touch.

With her fingertips, Crystal caressed Wilma's face. "You don't need such skin. It's fine just as it is."

Wilma swallowed somewhat nervously as Crystal's palm slid along her jaw bone and over her throat. Wilma thought of the daisies she pressed against her cheek every summer.

"I'm seeing myself years from now," Crystal said. "I hope I'm as beautiful."

Harold had never said anything so touching to Wilma in all their years together.

Embarrassed by the praise, Wilma said, "You talk foolishly."

And then Crystal didn't talk at all. Featherlike, her lips brushed Wilma's. It was a light, searching kiss. She pulled away and asked, "May I look at your breasts?"

Wilma clutched the sheet again, tighter this time, and remained silent. She wished she could take a couple of Bufferin.

"Oh, Wilma," Crystal whispered. "What're you afraid I'll see?" She tugged slightly at the sheet.

With great reluctance, Wilma surrendered it.

Wilma's breasts lay flat and to each side of her chest. There was little natural lift to them anymore. She needed to wear a bra all day long or her chest muscles would ache. Her belly was too round and too high even when she lay flat as she was now. The skin on her upper arms wasn't tight anymore, and her thighs had ripples in them when she did her Richard Simmons exercises or bent forward or if she just stood still.

"What's this from?" Crystal asked. With fog-like softness, she drew her hand the length of Wilma's torso, down between her breasts, over her abdomen and onto the long pale scar curving around her navel and disappearing into her graying pubic hair.

Wilma's face flamed. "It was a long time ago. Cancer." She reached for the sheet, saying, "I don't think this is a good idea, Crystal." She had only an aging body to offer this young woman who didn't have a blotch on her.

Crystal's hand stopped Wilma as she bent to kiss the scar. Her hair tickled Wilma's chest and in a throaty voice she replied, "I do." Her tongue slid the length of the old wound, stopping at Wilma's hairline.

Wilma felt a muscle deep within her belly pleasantly constrict and then release itself. She wasn't ready for this and gently pushed Crystal's head aside.

Crystal moved back alongside Wilma, resting a resolute arm across Wilma's chest. She looked intently into the older woman's eyes. "You're really lovely, you know. You've traveled further than I have. One day I'll be battle-scarred by life, too. Won't you allow me to understand where I'll be?"

Wilma blinked several times. As though in a dream and as self-conscious as if on her very first date, she allowed Crystal to encircle her with her arms, which, Wilma thought, was a piddlin' little thing to do now that Crystal had kissed her mouth and her *belly.*

She closed her eyes, determined to get into the action, and drew Crystal to her. Crystal was so small and slender, almost elf-like, and as smooth as fresh cream.

Cautiously, Crystal positioned herself over Wilma. "You feel so wonderfully good."

Harold had never said anything like that.

Wilma ran her hands up and down the deep furrow of Crystal's spine. Her skin was silken. A flame ignited in Wilma's belly. Oh, she'd punish Harold a good one, all right, once she got through this ... this situation.

Crystal leaned close to Wilma's ear and breathed against her cheek. She kissed her earlobe, the sound of it barely audible.

A second surge of heat hit Wilma, lower this time, much lower. She heard her own breathing increase.

Crystal's lips met Wilma's again and with lazy, sensuous movement her tongue entered Wilma's mouth. Like a morning glory, Wilma fully opened her lips. The slow pressure of Crystal's lips increased and Wilma pulled her closer.

Crystal's hand glided along Wilma's face as she

pressed her cheek against Wilma's right breast. Wilma could feel surges of heat ripping through her body. Her heart was going out of rhythm. She ignored it, knowing it was nothing and yet everything because Crystal was responsible for its erratic behavior, and Wilma felt wanted.

Sweat built between their bodies wherever they touched which was everywhere as far as Wilma could tell. Tentatively, she cupped Crystal's breast in her hand. It was kitten-soft except for the nipple which felt like a granite pebble. She rubbed the hardened bulb between her fingertips and Crystal moaned.

Harold had never treated Wilma that way.

With her knee, Crystal spread Wilma's legs. There was some discomfort in Wilma's thighs, but if she didn't separate them further she'd be all right. "The light," she said.

Crystal turned it off.

"Another pillow, too."

Crystal's smile was visible by the street light filtering through the curtained window as Wilma tucked the support behind her head and shoulders. "Can't lay flat comfortably," she admitted.

"It's all right," Crystal said, and with jackhammer force, came down on Wilma's mouth.

Lava spread through Wilma's limbs. Her breasts had a mind of their own, and Wilma guided Crystal's hand to them. All that Wilma had brought into this bed with her was falling away like dead petals from a once fresh flower, leaving her able to bloom again, a different color this time, a different shape, a different blossom.

Crystal's fingers moved to Wilma's belly. They

slipped through soft curling hair and separated moist lips. Crystal began to stroke Wilma very slowly. "Petals," she murmured against Wilma's cheek.

"Yes, petals," Wilma breathed back. The very idea that they were having similar thoughts about flowers sent a thrill galloping through Wilma's breast.

The wider Crystal spread Wilma, the wetter Wilma became and the more she wanted to open her legs. She grasped her knees, pulling her legs against her chest. If there was the old familiar pain in her hips, she wasn't aware of it, and she languished in the clamorous flame of arousal Crystal was causing by touching her outside. Not inside, but *outside*.

Harold had never done that.

Now Crystal took Wilma's nipple in her mouth. It created a volcanic detonation in Wilma's crotch. Wilma knew if she shifted an inch she would explode into a million tiny pieces of molten tissue. She arched her hips as Crystal slowly rubbed her entire swollen fleshy area. "Slower, ah, slower," she gasped. "Make it last."

"You're so wet, darling," Crystal whispered, "so ready. Come now. We'll do it again in a moment."

Wilma came now. She came wildly, thrashing from side to side, her back bowed, her knees still held tight against her body, her clitoris flexing gloriously as thunderbolts of sensation arced through her. Sweat poured down the sides of her face and over her rib cage. Her hair was plastered against her forehead and cheeks. She gasped repeatedly, wrapped in glowing ecstasy.

Then gradually the room returned. Wilma could feel Crystal's fingers slip deep inside her. She flexed her inner muscles so that she could grab onto this astonishing lover. "Don't go anywhere." Her voice sounded garbled.

"Nowhere, my beloved, nowhere."

Wilma slowly released her legs, stretching out with cautious motion and then came to rest. Crystal leisurely withdrew her hand and Wilma sighed. Harold had never done *that!*

"You're right, Crystal," Wilma uttered. Her lips barely functioned.

"About what, darling?" Crystal whispered against her ear.

"I've never made love before."

"I'll give you my phone number."

"I'll take it."

B.B.'s Story

Phyllis Horn

Since you've asked, let me tell you about B.B. We struck up a friendship the summer after I got my second-hand Western Flyer for Christmas. I was lucky to get any kind of bike at all, for I was a Mill Hill kid, growing up on cotton mill property in the piedmont. No matter how you cut it, we were dirt poor. So was B.B. But neither one of us realized it then, and wouldn't have cared if we had.

It's hard to tell when any story *really* starts, but this one begins, I think, one day when I looked up and there's Barbara Brandon banging on our screen door. For a minute I wasn't sure it was her, because seventh graders steered clear of elementary school *babies* like I was, and she'd just been promoted. I squinted at her, and it was her all right, tall and yellow-haired. I yelled out, "Come on in, Brandon. Whatcha want?" Like I didn't care, you know.

She sauntered in, cleared her throat twice and said, "Girl." Like she didn't know my name. "Girl, I'm gonna ride my bike down to the creek. Maybe play some cards — or go wadin'. You can come if you want to. 'Less you're too much of a sissy to go that far. Your Mama let you go?"

That creek was strictly off limits to me. I considered that and decided I'd take my chances. "Sure. I can do stuff like that," I said. "I'm in the fifth grade next year."

She studied me with crystalline blue eyes that took in everything and told nothing as I informed my mother, "We wanna ride down to her house on our bikes and play for a while. Her mama's working the second shift this summer. She'll be there." Barbara nodded, swearing to the truth of it.

"We'll play in the shade where Mrs. Brandon can see us. Okay, Mom?" I pressed. A prickly rush ran suddenly through my chest even as I spoke. It hadn't really hit me until the moment I told that lie how it gave Barbara enough on me to make me her slave for as long as she wanted. She knew my mother would spank me good if she found out I didn't go where I said I was going. But Mom said yes before I could take it back.

Our days together that summer got to be high ritual. We'd go to the forbidden creek, lean our bicycles up against a tree, take in a deep, slow breath like we'd seen grown people do and drop down beside the water. I can smell that creek now if I try. It was a kind of heady, too-sweet smell, and it was cool in a way no machine can ever make water cool on a blazing summer day.

Somehow B.B.'d gotten hold of a regular deck of cards that had two sevens missing, so we'd play War, where missing cards didn't matter. She had a great memory and usually won, though I'd heard she didn't do very well in school.

She was full of surprises, B.B. was. Some days she'd hide one of those tiny little Cokes they don't make anymore under her shirt, and bring it to share with me. When she got real brave, she'd steal a pack of her daddy's Camels, then stick an onion in her pocket for us to eat so nobody would smell cigarettes on our breath. We'd play cards and smoke our brains out. I never stole anything myself, but if I earned some money doing ironing, I'd buy her something. I felt pretty grownup that summer.

But I had a lot to learn, and B.B. was ready to teach me. One Monday in July, I could feel her getting restless. She was sitting by the creek shuffling cards in that fancy way her uncle had taught her, with all kinds of falls and card cuts, while I stood still and ankle deep in the creek, searching for crawdads. "Hershey," she said in a whisper. (She'd started calling me that one day when I bought her a Hershey bar with almonds.) "You know what my daddy thinks about you?"

I looked up and frowned. I didn't know her daddy even knew I existed, but I was certain I didn't like him discussing me behind my back. I'd been practicing my swearing that week, working on combinations and variations, and I thought I was getting pretty good at it. So I said with as much swagger in my voice as I could muster, "What in hell makes you think I give a holy good goddamn what your daddy thinks? He don't know me from cat's shit."

She looked unimpressed. "He told my mother at the supper table last night that you look just like a boy and he thought I was in love with you," she said, and giggled.

"You're a friggin' liar," I said. "Girls can't fall in love with girls." I grabbed deep for a big crawdad that was trying to hide under a rock and missed it. "What'd you say back?"

"I didn't get a chance to say nothing. My brother like to've split his sides laughing. Mama made him leave the table and told my daddy to hush," she said. Then added sweetly, "I wish you *was* a boy."

We looked straight at each other for a long time ... at least it seemed like a long time to me ... before she started slowly dealing out a game of War on the wide flat place we'd cleared off and swept clean with pine branches.

"You know what happened to those tadpoles I caught last week and kept in a bucket?" I said, deliberately changing the subject.

"Oh, Hershey," she said, in her prissy, draw-yourself-up way. "I don't care nothin' about stupid tadpoles! Ya big baby! Don't you know anything?" She stared at me solemnly, like I was somebody with half a brain.

Without warning, my bottom lip started quivering

so bad I was afraid for a minute I might cry. "Shit, B.B.," I muttered. "You never like *nothing* I do!"

She looked at me real serious, like she was thinking about whether that might be true or not. Or if she cared. Suddenly she flashed me a smile like an angel's, and started dealing again. Maybe she was an angel. I can't say for sure she wasn't.

"I tell you what let's do," she said, putting the last card face down. "Whoever wins this game has to kiss the other one."

"Fucking-A," I swore. I'd heard that one from the man at the filling station that week. I had no idea what it meant, but it had a nice rhythm. "Now what would I want to do that for?"

She sucked in a deep breath, as if to draw on the very bottom of her patience. "If you'll do it, I'll show you something. You know what a pussy is?"

I sat down on the other side of the dirt card table and crossed my legs. "A cat, silly. Whatcha gonna show me?"

"You swear on your mother's grave you won't ever tell?"

I made a big cross with my fingers over my flat chest. "I swear," I said.

She searched her back pockets, then held out a square of cardboard about the size of a baseball card.

I reached for it so I could get a better look. I'd started getting just a bit nearsighted that year.

"*Jeeezus!*" I said, and whistled through my teeth. I'd caught a glimpse of my mother once or twice when she was getting out of the bathtub, but I hadn't seen anything like what was on that card.

The woman in the picture was sprawled out on a sofa, buck naked, with her legs spread apart, and she had her finger stuck inside herself.

"Jesus H. Christ," I said. "Where in hell'd you get *this?*"

"I swiped it out of my daddy's bureau drawer," she replied coolly. "He's got a lot of other stuff like that too. You know what a rubber is?"

I didn't, but I wasn't about to say so, so I just sat there staring at the picture and squirming like I had to go to the bathroom.

She stood up and leaned toward me so she could see the woman too. "Bet you've never seen no naked man's thing either."

"Piss up a rope, B.B., will you quit it! Let's play cards or I'm leavin'." I pitched the offending card at her like it was burning my hand.

She let out a high-pitched cackle that nearly choked her and hopped up and down. When she could stop hopping and coughing, she said, "Promise you'll kiss me if *you* win."

"What?" I said, sure she had lost her mind.

"Promise you'll kiss me if you win!"

"What the shit!" I grumbled. But it seemed like little enough price to pay to get her calmed down, and she usually won anyway, so I said, "All right, if you'll sit down and stop it. Just shut up. I think you've lost your marbles."

She flopped down across from me, all legs and arms, and picked up two of the cards she had dealt and took a look. Then she tossed them back onto the dirt table, face down, real fast so I couldn't see them.

"You're cheatin'," I said slowly. "Show me those damned cards. I'm supposed to see them before you turn 'em over."

I picked up the two cards she'd thrown away. Two tens. She should have kept them. They counted toward a win.

"Screw it!" I yelled at her. "You *are* cheating! You're supposed to keep pairs!"

"It's not cheatin' if I let you win. It's only cheatin' if you lose." She clutched her hands to her chest and rocked back and forth joyfully, like she had just discovered some paradox of the universe.

"You never let me win before! Why ya doin' it now?" I nearly screamed. I was so mad I forgot to swear.

"I never wanted you to kiss me before," she said, and put a big pucker on her face.

I slammed the cards down in the middle of the others and tried to jump up, but she grabbed hold of my jeans and held me.

"And I'm gonna do it," she said, and leaned over and planted a long one right on my mouth. When she finished, she sat back and grinned this smart-mouthed grin, like she'd really put one over on me.

"Nothing to that," I said, wiping my face across my arm. I tried not to appear taken aback, but I hadn't expected to like it.

"That ain't the only way to kiss," she said.

"What ain't the only way?" I said, shakily.

Before I knew what was happening, B.B. had moved crablike over to my side of the table and put her arm around my shoulder. "You *can* do it like this," she said. And with that, she planted another one on me. Only this time she stuck her tongue right in my mouth!

"Ugh!" I said and pulled away from her, spitting.

"You're a chickenshit," she said, looking at me with disgust. "You'd like it if you'd do it right. When I stick my tongue in there, you suck on it a little. It'll feel good."

Well, nobody called *me* chickenshit back then and got away with it, so I did what she said. And she was right. It did feel good. So good, in fact, something told me I wasn't supposed to like it as much as I did.

"Look," I told her when we finally separated, "we better be getting back now. My mama's gonna be looking for me. I gotta go." Then I shot her this goofy sort of grin so maybe she wouldn't get mad. I started to get up.

"Hershey, you ain't gotta go anywhere," she said and grabbed my pants again. "And if you don't shut up and do as I say, I'm gonna tell your mama where you been going all summer and your goose'll be really cooked."

My worst fears had happened!

"You better not," I said. But I knew she would and my mama'd beat the living daylights out of me twice. First for lying. Then again for going where she'd told me not to.

"Lie down," B.B. commanded. "I got somethin' else to show you."

Well, what could I do? I knew she had me, and so did she, so I stretched out in the dirt like she said, and lay there stiff as a board. "Like this?" I asked her.

She didn't answer, but got on top of me and started moving a little bit. Then she put her tongue back in my mouth and I started sucking.

We both got real excited by what we were doing and after a while we were breathing in quick, hot pants. She squirmed a little more, but I was too scared of what I was feeling to move. Finally she rolled off me and lay on her back on the ground.

"They call that dry fuckin'," she said. "I'm not for positive what that means, but I think it's nice. A girl in the eighth grade told me about it."

I swallowed a glob of dry spit that had come up in the back of my mouth and sat up. "Yeah," I said, "I think it's nice too. Can we please go now?"

We did it two or three more times that summer, if I remember right, and she never did tell my mama we'd been going down to the creek instead of to her house. Of course, I didn't tell anybody any of this for a long time.

Her old bicycle came up lame in early August and she started saving nickels for a new tire. School started before she had enough money, and she went off to Junior High and forgot I existed. I'd see her now and then with her arm around some pimply-faced boy from the Hill. Then we moved the next summer when my daddy got a better job in another mill.

But I never forgot her. And when people ask me how I think I came to be a lesbian, as you just did, I say, "God! Who knows? They say it's genetic."

Then I laugh and tell them about B.B.

Many Seas Away

Mary J. Jones

I knew a woman once, many seas away."

So Avalon's Sea-Daughters began their tales as
they stood, wind-burnt and handsome, in the Lady
Hall. Their harps glittered with salt from all the
oceans of the world and the treasure from their sea
bags covered the flagstone floor: bolts of Egyptian
cotton, double-headed Cretan axes, shields of black
and white hide — from a striped horse, they
claimed. Gems, too, with names as lovely as the

stones themselves: opal and obsidian, garnet and jade.

The Sea-Daughters sang of their adventures: *I knew a woman once ...* Many women, many adventures. With women who raced fleet horses across treeless steppes and women who trailed silk and scent through teak pagodas. They told of women covered foot to brow with the fur of Arctic wolves and those who ran naked and laughing beneath avenues of broad-leaved trees. Of women who wrought strange symbols with hollow sticks on tablets of damp clay. Of ebony-skinned women who ruled great nations from diamond-crusted thrones. Of tough, stringy warrior women whose shields fit tight over shorn left breasts and whose own stories were of the high, white walls of Troy.

Sometimes, the Daughters would name the women, the syllables spilling out into the Hall like jewels, too — Rosalinda and Ruth, Kama and Damaris, Keiko and Red Fawn. And then the Sea-Daughter who had known, say, Lioslath in Scotland or Amir in Arabia would speak of the luster of black hair or the taste of creamy flesh.

When I was a girl in the Child Corps, I went often to the feasts welcoming the Sea-Daughters home from their voyages. I would see the treasure and hear the stories. Afterward, I would lie on my barracks cot, pull the stiff wool blanket over my head and dream of adventures in some dark English forest or up north among the ice floes or on the hot, stinging sand of a distant shore. I would wish that

I, Ceara from dull little Tref Eithne, would one day
bring treasure to the Lady of the Lake and stand
before her to sing of a woman, many seas away.

And it came to pass. More or less. The Goddess,
our Mother, called me to be a Sea-Daughter of
Avalon. At fourteen I went to sea — in an old
carrack bound for the horse-fairs of the Celtic
Realms, though not with the sleek mares of the
Lady Line but a cargo of mules. That was my lot for
a long time, hardly the sort of thing around which
to weave bright strands of heroic saga or lacy tales
of beautiful women.

As the years went on, I became a solitary old
sea-dog in the service of the Lady of the Lake, hair
shot with gray and face the texture of a worn boot.
I also became less sailor than merchant, my life
wasted, I thought, in the boring business of striking
bargains with mainland men. But the Goddess put
the gift of gab in my sea bag and I had to use it
however the Lady saw fit. Late one summer she saw
fit for me to use it in Germany.

The Isle of Avalon, only just freed from years of
drought and disease, needed cash to buy new seed
and stock. What the Lady needed, in other words,
was a few fat nuggets of Teutonic gold. And for me
to get them. I threw up a certain amount of
resistance to the idea; no Daughter of Avalon had
ever dared journey to that land where the sky-father
was master and women his slaves. But the Lady's
orders were the Goddess's.

"To Germany it is, then," I said to the Island

messenger, Beitris of the Blue Harp, a Poet known for her especially lush songs of Lady-praise. "But where is this gold?"

"The river Rhine will lead you," Beitris said. "It cuts deep into that nation's soul."

A poet's reply, I thought, all metaphor and muddle. Nevertheless, I embarked for Germany.

Finding the gold might be a problem, but finding the river Rhine was certainly none. It spreads its entry to the sea over many leagues and among many peoples. It is also their high road of commerce. So I had no difficulty in hiring boat and crew, men who knew the river and, for a price, the way to its gold.

There were three of them. A rough lot, all covered with hair and dirt, but I like sailors, even the freshwater kind. And, since I showed myself an able and willing hand, these chaps liked me. I knew a bit of their language and pretty soon we were swapping songs and stories like old comrades. I told them about Maeve and Cuchulain. And they told me about the Rhine-gold.

It was a rather long tale and Kuonraet, their captain, explained that we would have to pull into shore while they told it. Reluctantly, I agreed and then spent half the day hearing about the Rhine-gold as the gift of the sky-father to the house of Hagen and how it was worth more than any other hoard in all the north.

I interrupted to ask if the current Hagen still held the treasure. I was assured he did — Hagen spent the sky-father's gift only on that for which it was intended.

"Which is?" I asked.

"War, of course," Kuonraet said. He added that Rheinfestung, Hagen's fortress, stood not far off.

"It is guarded, though, by the Rhinemaidens," Kuonraet said and suddenly his voice was full of fear.

I was impressed to know that Hagen could indeed afford the horses of the Lady Line. I wasn't so impressed by the gold's guardians, even when Kuonraet told me that if a man looked upon these Rhinemaidens he would turn to ice. I reminded him I was a woman.

The boatmen chewed on that a while and finally Kuonraet said, "Even so, you have come on a fool's errand. The gold will only leave Rheinfestung at Gotterdammerung."

"Gotterdammerung? And what is that?"

"The terrible time when the sky-father at last knows defeat," he said. "Then the universe will be consumed by fire and the gods themselves will perish in the flames."

Of all the superstitions I had encountered in a lifetime spent among strangers, I thought this one the most utterly savage.

But then the boatman added, "After Gotterdammerung, the Rhinemaidens will reclaim the gold from the ashes and spring will come again."

Another death and resurrection story. The world is full of them and generally their only purpose is to extort more money from the ignorant. I tossed Kuonraet a few more coins and shortly we were again gliding up the Rhine.

Nevertheless, a day or so later, when we approached the cliff atop which Hagen's fortress sat, it was clear the boatmen truly believed the Rhinemaidens would turn them to ice. Terrified, they clapped their hands over their eyes and threw themselves face down onto the deck. I, though, turned my own face to the high keep.

I saw nothing but cliff and, perhaps, the fleeting shadow of a figure among the rocks. The only sound was the sigh of pines, like the light laughter of a woman. A few miles on we pulled up to a jetty and the boatmen finally felt safe enough to thrust hairy arms toward the sky-father and cry out their guttural god-thanks. They did not bid me fair journey when I left them there, and I knew I would have to find a way out of Rheinfestung for myself.

A track led from the jetty up onto the clifftop and there joined a road that looked as if it had once been a king's highway now fallen into disuse. Weeds sprang up in the rubble of its paving and it was dark with overgrown bushes and untrimmed tree limbs. I am often nervous on land — I feel trapped by its enclosure — but this place frightened me especially. It was like a green winding sheet.

I gave a shout of thanks when at last I came to the broken gate of Rheinfestung. And there I stood shouting for some time, for no gate-keeper called welcome. I had just crawled over the fallen stockade when I glimpsed a spear-warrior striding toward me. I pressed my palms together and brought them to my lips in what would surely be a sign of peace even in this barbaric place.

The warrior, clad in a torn wool tunic, stopped and listened as I told my name, my nation, and my good intentions.

"Get out!" came the reply.

"And just who are you that you can turn me away from your lord's land?"

"Gyldan, the lord's daughter, though it is no concern of yours."

So this was one of the so-called Rhinemaidens. Well, Gyldan was hardly the pale dainty of the boatmen's tale; rather a strapping big woman, taller than I, with black hair and river-dark eyes. The boatmen may have been afraid to look at her, but I liked what I saw. I wanted to continue seeing it.

What Gyldan wanted I do not know, but quite unexpectedly she said, "Night is coming. You may spend it here. Tomorrow, however, you will be gone."

I had supposed Rheinfestung would be crowded with warriors and retainers; instead, it seemed empty of any life. No man or horse or even dog prowled its bare little courtyard. And it was dilapidated; not a mighty timbered fortress but a rotting wooden hulk. Outbuildings lay crumbling and the keep itself leaned like an old barn. In the great hall, moss clung to sagging beams, the only decoration a series of stuffed animal heads, mangy with age and neglect. A pair of guttering torches lit a carved oak table. The table had been scrubbed till it was white.

Gyldan bade me sit at it, on a leather camp stool, then disappeared. After a while, she returned, carrying a pair of drinking horns, and took a place at the table's far end. Then came a tiny gnome of a serving man, who set plates full of turnip in front of us and himself disappeared. The turnips were dry and the beer weak.

We ate in silence until at last Gyldan said, "What do you seek in my father's house?"

Now, I have been a merchant most of my life and know that there are some folk who like a bit of blarney before they do business. I judged, however, that Gyldan was not likely to be one of them. I got right down to it, telling her that Avalon wished to strike a bargain with Hagen. In trade for a bit of gold now the Lady would send, next summer, as many studs and mares of the Lady Line as Hagen might want. The offer wildly exceeded my orders, but this was no time to be mean.

"My father is not here. The gold is his," Gyldan said, not looking up from her plate. Her voice was strained and hollow; who knew when she last had used it.

"Then I will wait for him to return."

"Hagen honors no woman," she said, lifting her gaze to me. In her eyes was a clear warning. And, I thought, something else.

But before I could respond, she rose and went out of the hall. I was left to spend the night in my bedroll on the cold stone floor.

When I awoke the next morning, a storm raged over Rheinfestung, shaking its tattered timbers so fiercely I feared Gotterdammerung had truly come. And after that it was as if earth herself plotted to keep me there. Or so I told Gyldan. And, of course, she could see for herself that the autumn rain turned the river into a timber-clotted torrent and the road into a sucking black bog. Then came winter. Road, river froze then thawed, froze and thawed again. I claimed that not by boat or cart or foot could I find a way to be gone from Rheinfestung.

So Gyldan let me stay on, though I came to

wonder if her father's gold was worth the misery. For the weather was not the worst of it. Nor the food, though that was grim enough — salt pork, flat beer, dry turnips. It was the sheer boredom I feared I would perish of. Gyldan appeared only for the evening meal, during which she barely talked and after which she hied herself off to sleep away the long northern night. For weeks my sole companionship was the mounted heads of dead beasts. I began to wish even for the thin joys of Tref Eithne.

Finally, I reached the end of my endurance. I would make this silent woman speak. True, by then I hadn't many words myself — all my gab seemed to have left me — but I could still sing. And not just "*I knew a woman once ...*" I have half a hundred Island songs and twice that many sea-chanties, gypsy tales, and mainland romances. And I can belt them out in any key and nearly any language. It's a good talent to own, tale-singing, one that can loosen any tongue. And any purse.

At supper one night — and a wicked night it was, with a fierce ice-storm raging down the river — on that night, I began the story of the Rhine-gold. Just as I did, a noise arose in the courtyard — clattering hooves, barking dogs, shouting men. Out of the storm, Hagen had come home. He swept into the hall with a cold wind at his back and his warband by his side.

He was as dark as his daughter, but with a curved nose and hooded eyes lighter than his face. In a battle-bold voice he commanded his hearth-companions to join him at the table. The rest of the band, mail-clad men with eyes as gray and hard as their swords, ranged themselves against the rock walls.

Hagen drank down two horns of beer, watching me as he did so. Then he turned to Gyldan. "Who is this at my table?"

Before she could answer, I told him I was Ceara of Avalon, "Come to offer the great king Hagen horses. Strong horses to carry your conquering warriors against Frank and Slav alike. Many horses, my lord, and splendid enough to ride into Valhalla itself."

"And the price of these wondrous steeds?" His voice was a low hiss now, and I could see his wet, yellow teeth.

I explained about the Rhine-gold.

There was silence in the hall when I finished. Hagen stared at me for a while, then the corner of one lip curled into his mustache. "So this Avalon wants Rheinfestung's gold? And it sends a woman to get it? There is only one way for a woman to get gold," he said. "To be sold for it."

Island honor demands much of a Daughter but not that she be stupid. I took one look at the warband's drawn swords and surrendered. As a warrior led me out of the hall, I glanced at Gyldan. For a moment, our eyes caught and held. Then she looked away.

They threw me into a little outbuilding. It was bare rock except for a high, unglazed window which let in more cold than light; under it I shivered away my first night as a slave. In the morning, a bondsman brought a worn old blanket and a cracked slop jar. He also left a bit of bread and a scrap of frozen meat.

When my physical needs were met, I began trying to find a means of escape. For days, I clawed at the rock flooring, tried to crawl up the icy wall to the window, and once even attempted to overpower the bondsman when he came to empty the slop jar. But finally captivity began to work its evil; I fell into the lassitude that creates a slave more surely than does an iron chain. I began to smile at my captors and sing them the songs of home.

Soon, Hagen was allowing me to sing in his hall. He sat silently through these recitations, as did his daughter and warband, and when I was done he sent me away with neither thanks nor food. One evening, though, Gyldan thrust a cup of mulled wine into my hand. "Drink," she said without looking at me. "The night will be cold." In my cell, I found not my old blanket but the thick pelt of a black bear.

After that, it was often Gyldan who led me to and from the hall. We never spoke, but when I sometimes slipped on the ice of the courtyard — my ankles were shackled — she would catch me and her hand would linger on my arm.

And so I waited for, sang my way into slavery — until the loud cracking of the river ice told me spring was near. It was on a night warmed by some stray southern breeze that I came into an empty hall. Empty except for Gyldan.

Gone now was her torn wool tunic. She wore a linen gown splashed over with bright, golden embroidery. Her hair gleamed dark and rich in the torchlight.

"Where is Hagen?" I asked her. "And his men?"

"Gone warring," she said. "It's spring."

"Isn't he going to take his new slave to market?"

"Slaving is women's work."

The words froze me where I stood.

Gyldan bade me be seated at the oak table and served the supper herself, the bondsmen having apparently decamped with their lord. When we had eaten — in silence, of course — she commanded me to sing.

I began where Hagen's arrival had interrupted me those many months ago — with the story of the Rhine-gold. At first, I stumbled over the German but before long I was in full voice, wildly lamenting the twilight of the gods. Gyldan began to giggle.

I paused, sure she would soon remember her manners. I might be a slave now, but I was also a guest at her table. And of all the breaches of courtesy conceivable, the most loathsome for a Daughter of Avalon is to be giggled at.

Gyldan didn't stop, even when I began to sing again. In fact, she giggled harder. I could have tolerated an honest guffaw or two, but giggling? Never! Anyway, who would have taken this cool, silent woman for a . . . a giggler.

"What are you —" I couldn't even say the word — "laughing at?"

"That silly story and your terrible grammar," she said and giggled some more.

I put my hand to her mouth to stop the foolish sound. Our eyes met and beneath my fingers I felt her lips tremble, though not now with laughter. I drew her to me and we drank of each other like winter-seized earth drinks of spring rain. She struck off my shackles then and, later, in her bed, we came together in crashing cascades of desire until, toward dawn, we fell back, filled at last.

And so we spent the spring in the flood-tide of our love. Then one day a mail-clad rider appeared in the courtyard. "Tonight, our lord will return," he said. "He will spend only this one night here. There is battle to be waged in the east. But he brings with him the king of the Saxons and bids you have the slave ready for delivery to him."

The messenger rode off. Gyldan stood staring after him. I pulled her into my arms and, to my surprise, she began to weep. Then we both wept for a time and, finally, we talked. We talked more that day than in all the months I had been in Rheinfestung and when we finished, she took me to the Rhine-gold. I filled my sea bag to overflowing with it.

Hagen returned at dusk. While I hid near the old road and Gyldan served them, he, his men, and his allies drank and feasted late in the decaying hall. When they staggered off to bed, Gyldan took a torch and set fire to Rheinfestung. For a long time, we watched the flames light up the northern sky, until at last the blazing hulk fell in upon itself.

"Gotterdammerung," Gyldan said, then took my hand to begin the journey west, to Avalon, many seas away.

Come Here

Karin Kallmaker

This night is like any other. If I screen out the steady drone of traffic and the monotonous tick of the mantle clock, I hear the quiet drip of the fog that has blanketed our district of San Francisco for the last few days. I also hear the whisper of a page turning behind me. I don't turn to look. I know exactly how Dedric has sprawled in the armchair, her long legs hanging over one side. I know without looking that one slipper has fallen off; the other dangles from her toes. I shake this image of her from my mind and go back to my files.

My psychotherapy practice is thriving and the files are always in need of updating. I am breaking the rules by working on the night we choose every week as "date night." Dedric is immersed in the last pages of a spy thriller and so far hasn't said she minded my working. I set one file aside, my notes complete, and stretch lazily before taking another. I feel guilty for taking our special time and though the work needs to be done, I half wish she would remember it was date night and make me stop. There are many other ways I would like to spend the night: dancing in her arms, wrapped in a blanket with her in front of the fire, entwined in the softness of our bed.

The clock ticks as I finish two more files. The fog gathers closer and I no longer hear traffic on the street. I stretch again, running my hands over the small of my back, arching my shoulders. As I open another file I hear the soft thud of a book falling to the floor and the rustle of fabric as Dedric shifts position.

"Come here." Dedric's silken voice whispers over my ears.

The files become a blur. I have been under Dedric's unrelenting spell for nine years and those two words, in that voice of hers, never fail to find response in my body.

"Judy." Her voice is a low contralto. I have heard it raised in a forceful, commanding yell of, "Stop, police." But tonight her voice is soft, edged with the need that is her one weakness — her need for me.

I put down my pen, aware that her eyes are on

me. I put off meeting her gaze for I know when I do I will lose myself in the oceans of emerald green. My hands will lose themselves in her long, thick, auburn hair. My lips will be lost to her demanding passion. So I don't look at her, not yet.

I close the file on top and tidy the stacks, aware that I won't return to them until tomorrow. As a psychologist I understand why it is so important to me that I close the door on my professional life before opening the door to Dedric's love. My patients would not recognize their quiet, pillar-of-rock therapist as the woman who is trembling as she rises from the table, gaze unfocused, lips parted, breath quickened.

Dedric's features are cast in a soft Irish mold of creamy skin that sprouts freckles in the sun. When she's in uniform she pulls her masses of hair into a no-nonsense ponytail. The severity would make most women appear more angular, but it only emphasizes how her brows arch and the smooth rise of her throat. I know that she could have chosen anyone to be her mate, but she chose me. I am the only one who makes her more beautiful still. I am the only one who sees her goddess beauty amplified by passion and desire. I am the one she loves, the one she needs.

I am now in front of her as she looks up at me from the depths of the armchair. Just as my patients would not recognize my passion and surrender, her fellow officers would not recognize the flush on her cheeks, the hair down around her shoulders, the eyes that are pleading. They often accuse her of coldness. Among our friends she's regarded as an outrageously bawdy flirt. No one but

I knows these expressions on her face, this open posture of her body, the lips that have grown fuller and redder over the past minute as my gaze devoured their sweetness.

I slide onto her knee. I know my power over her. She has been decorated for her courage and strength, but at this moment I know she is in my complete control. Arms that can bench press one-eighty sweep around me, hold me helpless against the lushness of her body. And yet I feel her trembling. I kiss her softly, quickly.

"Come to bed with me," she says, simultaneously asking and ordering. She needs to be specific, she wants me to know that we aren't tickling or teasing, snuggling or cuddling — maybe later, but not now and not for a while. I've known that since she said, "Come here."

"Yes." I kiss her softly and quickly again. She draws her breath in sharply and rocks me back in her arms. Her lips find my throat and the sound of her mouth leaving warm and moist kisses is no louder than the tick of the clock, but it is a symphony to me. The sound of her lips on my body moves me more than the sight of it. She presses her mouth to my breasts, which are hard and arching in their confinement and I raise my hand to unbutton and expose but she stops me with a slight shake of the head.

"Not yet." Her mouth returns to them, torturing me with muffled nips and slow warmth. She tells me how soft I am to her mouth, how lovely I am to her, and then, raggedly, she says, "I want you so much."

I capture her hand, then draw it to me, inviting her to cup and stroke my answering ache through the soft fabric of my slacks. She slowly moves her palm between my legs, as slowly as her lips find mine again, as slowly as she opens my mouth and tastes me more deeply. Her breathing is faster now, her palm speeds up, rubbing me there as I thrust against it. Then her fingers press in.

I hold nothing back. She knows what she is doing to me and that I can't hold anything back. That is my power over her, that I can't resist her, that I can't get enough of her, that I want and need to take exactly what she wants and needs to give.

She is groaning as her fingers agitate me even more. "Inside," I plead. "Stop teasing." She hasn't been teasing — her touch has been direct. But she knows what I mean and her hand is under my clothing, cupping ... oh so cruel, now she teases me, making me pay for having falsely accused her. "I'm going to ... Dee, please, I want your fingers in me when I ..."

Supple, warm strokes fill me. She holds me tightly against her as I thrust myself to her, then cling. Not long ... not ... long. She knows how close I am. Her touch changes, shifts, finds those places that are fluttering and quivering. The stroke of her fingers tightens me. I'm stiffening ... I want to be fluid for her but I can't help myself. My legs are rigid now, my spine straightening. But her arm holds me close and cradles me when all the tautness and strain explodes and I crumple against her, cooing pet names and murmuring sweet everythings in her ear.

Her heartbeat and breathing are the only sounds I hear now. I revel in the peace that rolls over me. My work is forgotten, everything is gone. I could fall asleep in the cradle of her love, but her fingers shift slightly, then slide out of me. My hips follow them and the peace dissolves. My cooing becomes demanding. I seek the full swells under her shirt with my mouth. She doesn't stop me when I awkwardly, hurriedly unbutton her shirt. I'm fast and direct — not teasing — as I worship her breasts, savoring these heavy treasures that arch to meet my mouth.

The world shifts and after my vertigo subsides I realize she has stood up, still cradling me in her arms. She carries me down the hallway and kicks the bedroom door open. Then she sits me gently on the bed and stands before me. She would be intimidatingly strong if her hands weren't trembling on my shoulders as she clutches me to her for balance and out of desire, drawing my head to her breast, offering herself to my taste and pleasure.

The sight of her half-naked body excites me more than when she is completely nude. She is so lovely she becomes a statue, an art work, something I can't touch. Nine years ago we had nowhere to go to make love so we found places for quick fumblings — maybe that is what has stayed with me. Like this, her shirt open, her pale skin gleaming in the dim light — the pain of my desire makes me delirious. I know I'll remove all her clothing eventually, and I'll revel in her naked limbs and glorious softness. But now she is pushing me back. My mouth doesn't want to leave her taut and aroused breasts, but she pushes and I yield.

I yield my clothing, piece by piece, until nothing separates my body from her hungry, emerald eyes. She gathers her hair, arching her neck in aristocratic beauty as she does so, and with the thick hair she sweeps my body. Her hair is pure, heavy silk, whispering silk, like her voice. It raises goose pimples on my thighs and stomach, over my shoulders and arms.

Her hands are on me again. Now her teeth capture and tease my bare breasts, alternating loving bites with strokes of her tongue. I wind my hands in hair, losing them in the masses of silk and she looks up at me. I look into her eyes, oceans of emerald green; I am swept away.

She kneels between my trembling legs. My knees capture her hips. My hands, still wound in her hair, pull her down. Elegantly and slowly — a swan coming to a delicate rest on a still lake — she dives into my wetness, but I am not still, I am moving, moaning, gasping. When I let go of her hair it flows over my hips. I let go to fall back, to yield myself up, to show her how much I do need her. I am her weakness.

All the analysis in the world can't capture the essence of the exchange between us. I can never describe in objective terms what her tongue, slipping through my welcoming flesh, seeking into my most private and hungry places, does to me. It's jumping out of an airplane without a parachute, riding a roller coaster made of cotton. There are no words. Except hers. Small, crying words, pleading words gasped between kisses and strokes of her tongue until I give in, can't hold back. She crushes her mouth to me as I arch and cry out. Her strong arms slip under my body, cradling me as I hurtle at the speed of light to the place where she takes me.

When I return she is preening her satisfaction at

my satisfaction. She takes such pleasure in my pleasure that I could forget that she needs more pleasure than that. She protests as I move to her side, returning lazily to my abject worship of her breasts. Her protests become a sigh, her sigh a moan, and her moan fades to silence. I know her jaw is clenched. Her body becomes rigid. This is the barrier only I have climbed. She freezes with the fear that I will somehow be repulsed by the fragrance of her body, the sounds of her passion, the texture of her wetness. She revels in her sexual prowess but is scared of her sexual attraction. I start to talk. I tell her what I want to do. I tell her what I'm going to do. I tell her how much I want to. By the end of my speech I am so aroused I am rubbing myself against the sharp point of her hip bone. I pull her hand to me and show her what wanting her has done to me again.

Her body melts. I fly past her barriers, wrapping her long, muscular legs around my shoulders. Breathing her in, tasting her in shudders of pleasure, I moan to her my awe of her beautiful essence. I cover my lips with it, fill my mouth with it, ever conscious of her legs gripping me, her answering gasps breaking out of her lungs faster and faster. I take such pleasure in it that it seems the most selfish act possible.

We untangle our bodies. I try to move, to rejoin again but when I do I shake, so I rest. I close my eyes and drift. I love our tradition of date night.

In the morning, as is my habit, I will probably analyze why I put her actions and mine in those terms — weakness and need — and my analysis will examine my past experiences, my childhood, my lesbian nature. The analysis allows me to dwell in my working hours on how she loves me. In analytical terms I can consider what she does to me, what I do to her. I think if I confronted the sensations, the desire, the pleasure — the sounds, the wetness, the loving — any of that, away from her arms, in the light of day, I would never stop blushing, never stop shuddering, never stop wanting.

"Come here." Her voice caresses me in the darkness, stirring me again. I did. I do. I will.

City Slicker

Lee Lynch

Water Street in Arborville, New York backs onto the river. Adrian had spent the first part of her life on the south end of town, on Willow Lane. In spite of her big plans, at age thirty-seven north Water Street was as far as she'd gotten. She'd been brooding lately about the rest of her life.

This day she hadn't slept well and took a nap when she got home from work at 5:15. Little Champ woke her twenty minutes later yapping and then the guy next door came home and started fighting with his wife, so she decided to take Champ for her walk while there was a little bit of light left.

She shrugged into her new yellow nautical slicker, the one she'd wanted since the days she'd dreamed of going to sea, hooked up the dog and slammed the front door behind her, hoping to jar the Krepskis into consideration for their neighbors.

Outside there was just the sound of the river out back and when they reached the park across the street, the soggy shuffle of early fall leaves underfoot. Champ found a magnificent scent immediately and Adrian, still sleepy, swayed at her end of the leash, dreamily studying her house. It wasn't much, just a cottage, but really, when she thought about it, saving up to buy a house on what a hospital personnel assistant was paid around here was not all that mean a feat. So what if she'd never seen the seven wonders of the world. Home ownership was something she hadn't even imagined.

The rain, still spitting a moment ago, let up altogether. An old dark car whished by on the wet street. Champ was carefully lifting single stones and licking something gross from each. Adrian tugged at the dog, but at the corner Champ paused again. Adrian's heart was thudding as if from great exertion. Her legs felt weak.

"This may not be a long walk, Champ," she said. "I think it's time for dinner." She knew, though, that she wasn't hungry for food. There was something else inside her, beating through her veins, seeking its own satisfaction. She turned away from their usual route down by the river.

The park took up a whole block. The black iron fence around it needed repair. At the far end were

swings, seesaws, slides and a bright blue plastic
structure with spaces for little kids to crawl, climb
and hide. Benches lined the intersecting paths. In
the twilight, after the rain, no one sat on them, no
one played, no one else walked except a lone figure
entering by the swings. Adrian had a nervous fear of
meeting up with the person, who strolled, hands
deep in the pockets of a trench coat, head down.

They could head back home, to the river, speed
up around the park, but she had a feeling that
whatever decision she made would bring her closer
to the intrusive stranger just that much sooner. That
was ridiculous, she decided, and let Champ set the
pace. Her heart was still thudding, her forehead felt
damp, her hands trembly. The rain hadn't cleared
the air,which was muggy and heavy with the smell
of decaying leaves and pollution from the factories
over in Binghamton. The figure, seemingly oblivious,
was headed their way. Champ pulled, eager for the
meeting. Adrian dragged her feet, but sneaked a
look.

It was then that the woman raised her gaze.
They both stopped short.

"Yolanda!"

"Adrian Landers!"

"I thought you moved to New York. After
college," Adrian stammered. Was this what all the
thudding and sweating was about? Had she sensed
Yolanda's presence?

"Dad's not well."

"I'm sorry."

"My brother owns a place on the other side of
the park. That three-story brick box. He rents out
the first and third floors."

Adrian showed off her house. They fell silent. Champ strained at her leash, just short of Yolanda.

"Cute dog. What is it?"

"Oh, you know, a little of this, a little of that. Mostly terrier I guess."

"So are you visiting too? I thought you were going to hop a freighter and sail around the world till you found —"

She shook her head. "I was twenty, Yolanda. I thought I could work a couple of years, save the money, you know. But things happened."

Yolanda smiled. She was beautiful, just as she'd always been. There'd been times back then when Adrian had thought she'd do an old-fashioned swoon just at the sight of her, that sunny blond hair falling in a short glossy sixties mop around her face, that solid yet feminine figure with the strokable-looking breasts and hips.

The tingling, strange feelings had reached her head. She was hot. "Want to sit for a while?" she asked, moving to a nearby bench.

Yolanda hesitated. "This coat'll soak through in a minute."

"Here then." She swept off her new slicker, spread it on the bench, then realized the mistake she'd made. Women didn't do that sort of cavalier thing, especially for former would-be flames. "You city types aren't used to the elements," she joked to cover her confusion. "You are living in New York?" She didn't really have to ask. Yolanda had that shiny, up-to-date look about her. Adrian, in jeans, running shoes and a hooded S.U.N.Y. sweatshirt, felt like a hick.

"Yes," Yolanda said, lifting the heavy dark hair

from her neck with the most feminine of gestures. Her eyes had a new luster to them. Back then she'd looked like a kitten, as if everything was new and fascinating, from Adrian's sleek racing bike to the taste of the tart green apples that grew in Yolanda's Willow Street yard, right next door. Now she looked like she'd seen everything at least once and wanted to again. "Coming back here is like time travel."

"Arborville doesn't change."

Yolanda lowered those eyes of wonder. "People do." Champ sat panting at Yolanda as if anxious for what would come next. "Remember that last letter you wrote me? About being gay?" Yolanda asked.

Adrian felt like she was choking. Did she have to bring it up? She'd been mortified ever since.

"I'm sorry I never answered you. It took a long time to sink in." She looked up and into Adrian's eyes. "I freaked, to tell you the truth. I felt so sorry for you."

Adrian turned away. Except for the ever-moving river Arborville was intensely still. No breeze ruffled the leaves in the park trees, no traffic came by, she could hear her stomach growl.

"No," said Yolanda, reaching for her hand. "I'm ashamed now. I've wanted to write ever since I came out."

"You?" She withdrew her hand, using it to gesture her amazement. "You were so straight!"

How tormented her nights had turned when, in high school, the boys had come by to see Yolanda next door, lounging on the front porch, laughing with their hoarse changing voices at parties in Yolanda's yard, saying endless silent goodnights just out of sight.

"You know how it is, Adrian. I did what I was supposed to do. I didn't know how to be a free spirit like you."

Free spirit? She couldn't look at Yolanda. Should she tell her how she'd felt? She bent and picked up a rock. "Want this, girl?" she asked Champ and let her off her leash. She threw the rock almost to the other side of the park and realized the evening was growing dark. Should she ask Yolanda back to her house? "What do you do in New York?" she asked instead, irrelevantly.

"I draw ads."

"Anything I've seen?"

"Not unless you get technical catalogues. Or — unless you live with someone who does."

She smiled. "I live alone. I'm afraid I'm more bark than bite," she explained as Champ dropped the rock at her feet. She picked it up and threw it again. "I only had that one lover. We were together quite a while, but I didn't have what it takes to go hunting for another."

"So what do you do?"

"With my life? I visit the folks. Volunteer at the Women's Crisis Center. Play on the hospital softball team. Fix up my house. Work as many hours as I can get. In the good weather I take long bike rides."

"No, Ade, I meant for love, for sex."

The streetlights went on, pop, pop, pop, one block at a time.

"You haven't changed, have you?" said Adrian softly.

"Meaning?"

"I could always see the truth ready to jump out

of your eyes." Even in the dusky light of oncoming
night, of the years in between, Yolanda's eyes were
the blue of an open wildflower.

"It's the only way I know to get answers, asking."

"To tell you the truth, then, I don't do sex."

"And all these years I pictured you —"

"You thought of me?"

"Adrian, your letter was my first step in coming
out. You brought me out."

Champ sighed and scrambled up on the bench by
her side, but not between them, as if she'd
recognized that the conversation had just reached a
point of no return.

She took a deep breath, but didn't say, *I
certainly wanted to.* Would her life have been
radically different? There would have been no
question of settling down with Yolanda. A stable
career wouldn't have been uppermost in her mind.
There would have been a time of flaring excitement,
then of roots seared off. They wouldn't have stayed
together, but the experience would have driven her,
its pain or the need to match its high wire
excitement, out of Arborville, maybe onto her
freighters, or at least through America, looking for
more heights.

It was funny how the streetlamps made the park
feel as enclosed as a living room. "How did you
picture me?" she asked, stretching her legs out,
hearing the smile in her own voice.

Without hesitation Yolanda said, "In charge.
Hungry but controlled. Big and fun and passionate."

She laughed. "Maybe if I could live up to all that
I would do sex."

"What about me?" Yolanda asked.

Adrian was flustered. Was she supposed to ask Yolanda about her sex life?

Yolanda helped a little. "When I tell a woman, especially a straight one, that I'm gay, I'm usually doing more than giving information."

"Did I have an ulterior motive, you mean?" Those wide open eyes again, pulling the truth from her. "Did I want you, you mean? Did I expect you to drop all your little boys and see the light? Did I think you were in a different ballpark from them and your parents' rules?"

Yolanda's eyes said something else now. They were playing, watching Adrian's discomfort. Adrian's heart wouldn't stop pounding, she had to look down and catch her breath. Yolanda's hand caught her gaze, a small stubby-fingered hand with polished nails. A black bracelet edged in silver slid down from the trench coat's sleeve. Yolanda cared about those hands, dressed them up. What would their touch have been like?

She talked to the hand. "I was more focused on my desire than on your response. I was twenty, a walking hormone. You'd be soft, excited, weak-legged. I'd hold you up, then lay you down. You'd quiver."

"Mmm," said Yolanda, her hand clasping air in her fist, the warm muggy air that should have left with the rain.

"Who do you live with?" asked Adrian.

"Cara. We're very compatible except for sex, but the apartment is rent-controlled. Otherwise I'd be gone."

"You're still together?"

"She is. I'm not. She won't give up, but I did."

"That must be —"

"Uncomfortable. The solution's slow in coming." Yolanda shifted, crossed her legs. She was wearing nylons. Adrian shut out an image of them way up her thighs, attached to garters. "I play safe, though. Have you been tested?"

"I'd never have thought of it, but the hospital leaned on all the personnel. I like my job. I was negative twice and haven't been with anyone since."

"I'm negative too."

There wasn't even a breeze to rattle the leaves, to shake them down, to fill the silence. She wanted to flee, she wanted to know everything in between, she wanted there to have been nothing since they'd last met. She wanted to look at Yolanda with her own honest eyes. Would there be desire in them? Did she still want Yolanda, this Yolanda? The trembling was no longer just a feeling, tremors shook her hands, her innards.

"What else do you do?" she asked. "Besides your job."

"I have fun," answered Yolanda. "I've always been best at that."

"It must be easier to find in the city."

"No. I have to make my own entertainment there too." Yolanda moved closer. "You, for example," she said, touching Adrian's collar with a fingertip, "could be fun."

"Right. Fun and games in Water Street Park. I should've brought Champ's frisbee."

"Don't put yourself down. You were a lot of fun when we were kids."

Oh, no, she thought. That swooning feeling, the one she hadn't felt since high school, was back. She remembered Yolanda in a summer playsuit nimbly jumping from square to square playing hopscotch. She remembered ripe, exuberant Yolanda as a cheerleader in a tight sweater, and a short, short skirt.

"You always led the games we played as kids."

"You called me Yonda because you couldn't pronounce my name."

She stopped avoiding Yolanda's eyes, touched with her lips the knuckles of the hand that toyed with her collar. "Yonda."

"I like it."

"Do you want to come see my playhouse?"

"No. I want to have fun in Water Street Park."

"Listen, I —"

"I know. The neighbors. Your job. Kiss me, Adrian."

How long had it been? What was she really risking? How many years had she wanted this? Her old best friend Yonda, in the half-dark, wanting her.

"Again," said Yolanda after the first timid brush.

She kissed Yolanda, all the years of Yolanda, then put her arms around her. Now she shook seriously, all over. She pulled Yolanda tighter to steady herself. Yolanda played with the hairs on the back of her neck.

Adrian breathed her scent in. "I feel like a teenager, making out in the park."

"Let's be. Let's be seventeen and brash and careless with no place private to go."

"Oh, Yolanda."

"Come on, touch me like you want to, where you want to."

She kissed Yolanda's neck, as hot as the night.

They giggled when thunder cracked in the distance. "We may get wet," warned Adrian.

"We may, we may!" sang Yolanda, head back, eyes closed, drinking in her kisses.

"I've always loved you, Yonda."

Yolanda's voice had the carelessness of youth. "I love you too! Touch me, touch me!"

Adrian slipped a hand under the wide trench coat collar, unbuttoned a little round button, found the lace edging of a bra. "Yonda," she said, running her finger under the lace. Would the Krepskis call the police on her as she had on them that Saturday night? She didn't care. She opened all the little round buttons and reached back to open the bra.

"That's it, Adrian, yes," Yolanda said, biting her neck.

Oh, the intimacy of breasts, those soft heart cushions. She was crazed with their coolness in her hands, kissing Yolanda's lips like a starving person. She *was* a starving person. It'd been over ten years since she'd touched anyone like this. It'd been nearly thirty-seven since she'd first wanted to touch Yolanda. And Yolanda was nibbling at her lips now as she stroked the hard nipples.

"I'm so wet, Adrian."

"We can't," she replied. "Not here. Come to my house."

"No, Adrian. We're teenagers. We don't have a house. This is it. If we get caught we're in big trouble, but there's no stopping seventeen-year-olds. This is what should have happened then!"

"I can't, I can't," Adrian said, wanting the breasts in her mouth, wanting her lips on the smooth woman belly. "I want —"

"Think of what you wanted then. I'll bet some things weren't even in your vocabulary the first time. This is your first time too, isn't it?"

She laughed into the hollow of Yolanda's collarbone. "I knew nothing. I just went to the source," she said.

"*Do* it. Do you think I'll stop you?"

She stifled her own objections and, trying to cover Yolanda's legs with her trench coat, gathered her skirt, some sort of loose wide fabric, until her hand was full of it, then pushed it up to Yolanda's crotch. Pantyhose; no bare thighs.

"Say the things you would have said," Yolanda pleaded, opening her legs as far as the coat would allow.

Adrian worked her hand under the pantyhose. They were tight, she was afraid of running them. "We'll go to the same college," she said. Would that have been romantic then? "We'll room together. We'll push our beds together and get an apartment after we graduate."

"But, your freighters," protested Yolanda, gasping as Adrian's hand reached her sopping vulva. "Your world adventures."

"Come with me, then. We'll go together."

"Tell me."

"I love you so much, Yonda. I can't talk. I —"

"Tell me."

"We'll get work on cruise ships. You wouldn't be safe on a freighter. You couldn't do that kind of work. You'll be a maid, I'll be cook's helper. We'll share a cabin, sleep in the same —"

"Oh, Adrian, I think I'm coming. Is this what it's like?"

"The same bunk, Yonda, all naked and —"

"Yes," came the harsh explosion of breath from Yolanda, squirming under her hand.

Adrian held tight to her, keeping her still, covering her, never stopping her fingers.

Yolanda, cheerleader, hopscotch jumper, glossy city woman, looked up at her, eyes filled with the wonder of first sex.

Yolanda's breathing slowed. Adrian moved back to let her straighten her clothes. Champ still slept.

"My brother will be wondering," Yolanda said, kissing her.

"Call him from —"

"No. I'll sneak out later. My window's on the ground floor."

"Just tell him. We're adults."

Yolanda's eyes sparkled. "Oh, no we're not."

"I can come to you."

Yolanda sat up and pulled away. She pouted. How many times had she gotten her way with that pout! "You promised me a cabin. Bunk beds. I always wanted you to ask me to come away with you."

"But I'm not going —"

"You promised."

She thought of her bedroom over the noisy river. The back door that led right to it. A dormant sense of play flared in her like the streetlamps. Pop. Pop. Pop. The swooning came not so much from this woman now as from the wide horizon, once again in sight. She stood, pulled Yolanda to her. "Come tonight. When you can get away. You know which cabin? Around back. I'll be waiting."

She watched Yolanda, a flashing yellow-slickered figure, hurry back across the park, stop, wave like an over-excited kid, and cross the street.

Slicks

Vicki P. McConnell

She felt like a femme, cruising through all the piles of lingerie on the perfumey middle floor of this uppity department store. She was looking for something without lace edging, something devoid of queer portholes. She would know it by touch, and then her lover would know it by surprise.

The search took hours, her head began to swim, all this confection made her despair. She dove her fist into a last powdery pile — oh for narwhal hide amidst these tropical feather fish, oh for a single prize, slippery and black as if cut from a manta's cape. But her fingers did not close upon delivery.

Girlie panties would not suffice. She knew what she must do.

She'd seen the catalog at her friend Jeff's — all those insert pages, all those suntanned and sun-moist male models, photo after photo of ... *boys in briefs.* Perhaps she could find her prize there, just one pair without the gauzy sock in front or that silly tuck of stitches ...

She drove to the store in West L.A. Of course other womyn had shopped here proudly before her, but let them not be around today. Taking a deep breath, she crossed the threshold under the sign, *International Male.*

She pretended to browse perfect stacks of green and purple sweater vests. The clerks smiled at her as though she belonged. A glance toward open cases on her left revealed the goods she sought. No turning back now ... she stepped into the unknown world of Briefwear Galore, welcomed by rows and rows of slinky Boy-Bikinis, thongs, shortcuts, and something exotic called a fundoshi, all of them colorful as flags of state — red, yellow, sky blue, royal blue, emerald, teal, turquoise, periwinkle, stone-washed and striped. Some of the underwear had insignias — Fireman, Policeman, even camouflage for Soldier fantasies. But she did not want to feel like a fireman, she wanted the simple black surprise cut for the full bun, nothing French and high so the leg wandered on its own. She had hips, after all, wide and hard from her genetic line of stone haulers, a millennium of creative slaves who broke their hips in the sockets to build history.

She passed each tray, touching the cellophane packages of underwear with just her fingertip. Men's underwear, but what made it for *men,* really? She could claim the sturdy clean lines for herself, the strong seams and bold colors, who would see, who would know, except the one she trusted with her heart? Soon she was humming, all her reticence gone, a smile of hope beginning to form.

At the turn of the aisle, in a crinkly forest of parachute shorts, she found her bounty. *No-fly briefs* — in black silk, so thin, called onionskins — and more wonder, an undershirt to match.

From the first time she put them on, she knew her choice had been right. To herself, she called the underwear her "slicks," this fluid new armor underneath her clothing, worn to fool the rest of the world, people who thought they knew her and saw her by clear categories. To them she was Wit Lyde — female and normal and compliant under pressure. Wit laughed at them with the mouth between her legs. She judged them with the eyes set wide apart in each wing of her pelvis, eyes that could see everything better than infrared, her Braille eyes, brain eyes, lover's eyes now veiled by the cocoon of slicks. She wore them to slide away from prejudice and doubt, to slide into her lover's desire.

In other times, had she been stripped down for whipping, her tormentors would have gasped to come upon this secret underpinning. Like some banner of rebellion, like she wore some sign of the darker arts. Even now her second skin defied the role her own

people had assigned. They thought they knew her,
and saw her by clear categories. She was Wit Lyde
— butch, soft butch, made for boxer shorts, made for
flipping. In her slicks, she could slide away from this
judgement, slide into her own power.

Wit pushed her breasts against the smooth black
fabric of the undershirt, felt the way it wound
around her pecs. Indeed she bought the slicks for
this caress, for the silky blush rubbed at her own
nipple and hip, yes, but more for that discovery
when her lover would touch this new soft shell of
her. Would quaver, bewildered for a moment, then
recognize another veil between them dissolving, to
reveal ever more surrender. Wit dreamed of that
sharp stop in time when she would see the wet
widening of Marty's eyes, that pulse flaring in her
lover's throat, that glide of wonder upon the silk —
such was the true caress of homage sought. Wit
would have it, and Marty would give it.

The two of them weren't a scandal anymore, just
an anomaly. Only a few people still did double takes
now that she and Marty were no longer seen as
butch buddies who slept together just for bonding,
just to define territory. Still, Wit knew they
remained a mystery. She heard the femme whispers
over daiquiris and veggie dip at Sigourney's Lesbo
Bistro.

"What can two butches do?"

"Probably nothing, neither can give permission."

Wit remembered keenly the unexpected first
flirtation. In a crowded bar, no less, where signals
often cross and mean nothing, where confusion is a
constant, vulnerability too plain, too desperate, or
desperately denied. She and Marty had seemed to

have the same mission — to stand somehow within this giant flux of emotion and yet relax, flex their wings of confidence. Wit saw this strength in Marty's face at once, knew it when she smiled — nothing vacant or false. Knew it when they simply stood next to each other breathing, cool, calm, in, out, soft, strong.

Wit had noticed Marty's small hands, and the way she tapped the top of her club soda, then pressed the wedge of lemon against the cold glass. The moment gave Wit another image, that of tipping a sun-warmed pitcher of lemon-scented water over Marty's hair and naked back. As their shoulders touched briefly — an accident, no accident — they were both amused, yet refused to do the clichéd poses, none of that I-take-my-space-by-gawd, none of that butch ego sniping and word wrestling, or worse, those faux macho sounds and strides.

In a patch of salt poured on the black bar top, Marty made playful designs, her little finger tracing first a triangle, then a fleur-de-lis. When she had caught Wit's eye, she made Runic symbols: an arrow, meaning Teiwaz or victory in battle, then an X.

"Is that Gebo?" Wit guessed. "Meaning offerings from the gods?"

Marty nodded.

"Is this a test?" Wit smiled.

Marty smiled back. "All of life's a test, don't you think?" Her eyes swept the bar, showing a light deep and kind as she took in the whole of it and all the other womyn, like passing energy through a sieve. She made a plus sign in the salt, watched Wit watching her. Erased the cross simple as Etch-A-Sketch and made a dash, or negative sign.

"Some tests are about life and death." She claimed Wit's eyes. "I take those regularly. How about you?"

It took a moment before Wit understood. No one had ever offered her safety first — not about sex or the soul or even in friendship. But here was Marty seducing her with subtlety about an AIDS test. Valor before lust — Marty might as well have turned open her wrist and given blood to prove her honorable intentions. Wit ran her fingers over one of Marty's hands, over those small strong bones of the wrist, then turned the other woman's palm over. She traced her own dash sign against Marty's skin, felt the charge between them fast and heavy as free weights dropped on a live wire. "Some tests are about love," she said.

They both liked the windows open, wide open. The candles always made Wit think they had pitched a tent in some past life. They lolled together on the bed and talked of their unspectacular day and laughed about the flirtatious mailman. Marty wore a tight yellow muscle-tee. Wit stroked the outline of her arm.

"You work out today?"

"Wednesday is always good — not too many guys around the gym. I can grade up my weights without any *advice*."

Wit curled her hand around Marty's bicep, felt it harden like a kiss back to her touch. "You're getting bigger all the time." She didn't mean just in muscle bulk. Marty had this way of arching her shoulders and turning her head, as if she'd just sighed and shifted the planet she was carrying, the planet of Wit's own heart. Wit liked Marty naked except for the muscle shirt, liked the V of pleasure sweat that seeped through the fabric between her breasts. The wetting was a sign that Marty had opened there, had given her power more room in the cage of bones.

The candlelight flared as if fed from within their room. Marty traced Wit's face, then cupped her hand at the back of Wit's head, fingers winding into her hair. She pulled, met the first resistance, respected it. Made Wit's eyes tell her line by line in the liquid melting light ... *butch, my butch, top to my top, partner, equal, take, turntake, lift, hold, flex me, sex me, move what is heavy off my heart.*

They moved together, wrestle and press, harder tenderness, Wit's elbow braced against the bedstead, her knees locking. Marty's hand in command snapped open the jeans buttons one at a time. They laughed and pushed each other gently, more in play than test. Side by side, their might and will at match, each began to feel the veils that begged to slide away. They made this dive into safety together — each giving up nothing of the self but everything of fear and control.

"You ..."

"No, you ..."

"Okay."

"All right."

The roll of Marty's breath at Wit's ear made the long muscles in her legs twang, made her laugh into the sweet bower of their sturdy arms. Such arms could hold any hurt, could they not, why would she ever steel herself from Marty, even in anger or pain?

A wall of chain mail seemed to fall away inside her chest.

They pulled each other closer, Wit about to offer and receive the most divine caress, the revelation of the new black silk. What would Marty do or say, would she laugh or gasp, go speechless, go limp and be taken more quickly? Or would she resist and challenge, bite and tug and tear the new slick flag to shreds? Just as Wit's hand breached Marty's white shorts, Marty slid her own hand into Wit's Levis. Both crested upon the same intent, fingers sliding, seeking. Then they *both* found a wet and sleek surprise.

Wit laughed in recognition, her fingers balling up the silk of *Marty's* new underwear. She pressed the soft hot cloth across the frame of her lover's hips. Had they picked the same color? Had they nearly crossed paths going to that same store, searching out their own insignia? The silk flowed in her hand, thin as onionskin, warm as Marty's own skin now slippery and urging her touch.

Marty breathed a word into Wit's ear, into her heart, so soft she barely heard it, private as the calling drum and tone of sea bells. She peeled back the renascent silk shell easy as a slipknot. "Slicks," Wit whispered back, and slid the ladder of her lover's soul.

Who Is This Woman?

Isabel Miller

I hate to see women lonely, so I give up an evening
to bring together Marnie, who is having a run of
bad luck and is temporarily lonely, and Pat, who
always is. Well, actually I'm trying to get rid of Pat.
She wears a "Re-Elect President Nixon" button. She's
been calling me ever since I left Elise. Now I see
what Elise was good for — she scared off people like
Pat.

Marnie and Pat are not attracted, but they do go

on seeing a little of each other. They'd better, after the trouble I've gone to for them.

"How's it going with Pat?" I ask Marnie every week after our Consciousness-Raising meeting. "What's happening?"

Marnie and I both live in the Village and walk in the same direction. C-R makes me want to be simple and sincere. I always wear my glasses.

"Nothing," Marnie always says. "We went to a movie."

I ask, "Did you leap on her?"

"I don't *want* to leap on her," Marnie says. At first I mistake this for criticism of my matchmaking and am not pleased, but then I see that Marnie, though a big, tall, blue-jeany, striding woman, is a femme. Our C-R group has decreed that there's no such person.

Something about a big butchy femme just seizes my heart, and I take another look at Marnie and allow into my consciousness what I must have known all along, that Marnie looks something like my shrink, the infamous Nadine, that big klutzy aloof old peasant who has been ignoring my love-groans and tears and importunities for years and ruthlessly forcing me back to look again at my own shadow, as though she never heard of countertransference.

Within two or three years, Marnie will be an exact duplicate of Nadine. And Marnie is femme. And — now I know — so is Nadine. I've been going at her all wrong.

*   *   *   *   *

"Have you leapt on Pat yet?"

"Uh, no."

"Oh, Marnie, you're hopeless!" I say, and then —
because what's the good of freedom if I don't exercise
it? — I add, "*I'll* be your butch!"

I love Marnie for not laughing. She who finds so
much in life to laugh at does not laugh.

"I could go for that," she says.

"I really will. We'll act out any fantasy you
want."

"Oh, Lynn, I don't fantasize. Except hugs and
kisses. Never scenes."

"Think of one and we'll do it. Anything."

"Have you been thinking about your fantasy?
Remember, *anything.*"

"I had some trouble with it, so I asked this poet
I know, this gay guy, to help me. And he suggested
Hitchhiker."

"*Hitch*hiker?"

"I'm driving along and I pick up this hitchhiker
and I say I just left a date who wouldn't put out
and I'm in great discomfort —"

"Oh, God, it's so *masculine!*"

"I thought so too. I asked for a better one. So he
suggested Gas Station."

"Is it any better?"

"Not really. It's much the same, except that it
starts out 'Fill 'er up.' "

"Really, Marnie, when I offer you *any*thing, I do expect a little imagination, a little creativity. I mean, please spare me mute gazes and a grunt."

"Yes, I wanted something worthy. That's why I consulted the foremost creative mind of our time."

"I shudder to think of his poems if this is his idea of romance."

"They're wonderful. And he did suggest one pretty good fantasy."

"I'm not hopeful. His record is awful."

"He suggested Avon Lady."

"Oh, God, Avon products are so *cheap*. Avon Ladies are so *ugly*. It's not worthy."

"Wait, Lynn. *See* it. The doorbell goes *bing*-BONG. In comes this lovely fragrant woman, who slowly opens her mysterious case. She studies my hair and applies a product that will give it body and sheen. She shows me how to remove all individuality from my face. She layers it with wet makeup on a little white sponge and huffs and puffs it dry. She powders and rouges it. She makes little test dots of lipstick up and down my person. She eyelines and mascaras and deodorizes. Maybe she even has something for that telltale special odor that's becoming noticeable."

"But it's *Avon*. I can't stand Avon."

"Choose your favorite. It doesn't have to be Avon."

I'm not interested. Marnie has blown it. I offer her anything on earth or in heaven — history or a space ship, scenes from plays, Sappho with her favorite on Lesbos, Queen Anne and Sarah Churchill, Virginia Woolf behaving disgracefully on Vita

Sackville's couch, Eleanor Roosevelt and Lorena
Hickok romping in the White House, missing the
Inauguration Ball — and this is what Marnie comes
up with and it's not even her own idea. She may be
a superb healer and herbalist, but her mind is one
gray block after another, plodding grayly on large
gray feet.

But nobody else will let me be butch. Marnie will
not fall out of bed laughing if I try, the way Elise
did. I didn't even know Elise *could* laugh. With
Marnie I can become the world's greatest butch.
Infamous Nadine will forget her oath. She'll be the
weeper and pleader then, and I'll be so much finer
than she deserves. I will not take revenge on that
sparse gray hair, those huge blobby breasts, that
wattled throat. I will adore and worship them.

First I have to learn to be masterful. I need to
practice confident touch. I need to learn to start
things. It's good that Marnie isn't reminding me that
I promised her *anything*. She understands me. She
can roll with my changes, not hold me to the whim
of the moment, not be constantly hurt. I'm so tired
of people who take me seriously and get hurt and
whine *you promised* and *you said* and *what about
me?* and *don't you know who I am?* and all that
archetypal stuff. Marnie knows I'm a crowd, and
likes us all.

I say, "How about this? You're an aging actress
trying to make a comeback. I'm your dresser."

"I'd have to get a new bathrobe."

"Yes. I suggest a blue and white cotton kimono
with slits under the sleeves. And you're very scared.
And I'm doing your hair and making you up and

telling you you're great and I have to go to great lengths to reassure you that you're still the champ, still the most beautiful and intoxicating and evocative woman in the world. I stop at nothing."

"I like it."

"Good. Next Saturday night. A week from tomorrow. As soon as the Sunday *Times* hits the street, around nine. I like raspberry yogurt and the *Times* puzzle for breakfast."

"Marnie? It's Lynn," I say. "I'm so disappointed. Can you believe who's in town for the weekend, unannounced? My Uncle Joe!"

"I'm disappointed too. But I've got a clean apartment and a nifty new kimono, and all you've got is Uncle Joe."

"Well, to tell the truth —"

"No need."

"— the infamous Nadine, surly rotten mean nasty Nadine, has forbidden me. *Why did I tell her*? She says no one whose grasp on reality is as shaky as mine — what a bitch! — no one like me has any business playing a game that deliberately obliterates reality. She actually said — I can't believe it! — she said the best guide is still the Ten Commandments. I told her I'm batting about five hundred on them. I've coveted an occasional wife, but never an ox. She wants me to go back to Elise. She's determined to kill my Elf. She wants me to go through life the way she does, plodding grayly on large gray feet."

* * * * *

"So who are we?"

"You are Marnie and I am Lynn."

"A minute ago when I looked out my window and saw you in your beautiful coat paying your cab driver, I thought I was young George Gershwin on the Lower East Side being visited by the gorgeous Uptown Gentile lady who recognizes his genius."

"No, you are Marnie."

And now it's time to leap, and all I want to do is sit in Marnie's lap with my ear against her chest. Well, who's in charge here? I lead her to the couch, climb into her big soft lap, and put my cheek against her. "Talk to me!" I command, butchily, because I want to hear her voice vibrate her ribs. "Tell me about when you were a little girl. When I was a little girl I was standing on a table in the solarium in a pretty new dress and my mother and all my aunts and the seamstress were there saying how cute I was, how adorable, and then a cab pulled up. It was my father home from the war, and all my women ran to him and left me on the table. I couldn't get down. I've spent my life trying to get my women back. Talk to me. I've always wanted to know someone like you, whose parents didn't put all their unlived life on her. Talk to me. I feel so safe with you. My mother whipped me with a rosebush branch, with thorns, because I smelled of candy. The maid was so shocked. She said, 'How you treat that child is worse than a dog,' and I hit the maid. What was that?"

"That was love."

"Talk to me. Is it all right to talk? You're not disappointed?"

"No. I like it."

"Your voice is so nice. My mother wanted me to be beautiful."

"You are."

"Wait till you see. You'll laugh. Before my makeup. It takes me forty-five minutes, but it's good. It looks like no makeup, even in sunlight. It's funny how people can't see past nice hair and good makeup and see the little shaved white mouse I really am."

"Can I watch the transformation?"

"I don't allow it. But yes, because you love whoever I am."

"Yes."

"Other people need illusion. My dog Rose carries her turds in her mouth and piles them under my bed. One time I was in bed with somebody who suddenly froze and said, 'What's that in the dog's mouth?' and I said, 'Oh, that's a Crunchy Bone. Put the Crunchy Bone under the bed, Rose.' But to you I think I could have said, 'A turd.' Could I?"

"Um hmm."

"I don't like any of my friends. I want a whole new circle of plain people. Peasant people. I laugh at cripples. Can you handle that?"

"I suppose they might like that better than averted eyes."

"But it's not laughing. It's hysteria. I can't stop. Could we kiss a little? Let me rephrase that. Kiss me, woman!"

How can anything be as soft as Marnie's mouth?

I say, "Would you mind a very gentle grope? My hand seems drawn there, just to rest. Would it disappoint you if it just rested?"

"No. I think people who can't stand not to have an orgasm are sort of primitive."

"That's because we're both hopelessly pre-genital."

"I bought some grapes. Want one?"

"An orgy!"

"Did you see in the *Times* about the orgy the police broke up? And what shocked the police was, they had grapes."

The grapes are fun. We slip them back and forth in kisses. I open Marnie's shirt and bra to see if her breast sags enough to hide a grape. It does. Mine doesn't.

I say, "If you were a spy, you could carry grapes this way. I'm supposed to be big and strong too, like you, but my mother won't let me. *Wouldn't* let me. I could now, of course. I feel I won't live to be old. I feel I'm going to be a cripple. I'll need a lot of money. Did you ask I Ching about us?"

"Yes. It said, 'Keeping Still, Mountain.' "

"Elise wants me back. She calls every day."

"Of course."

"Lots of people are attracted to me."

"I know."

"I hate it. It's a nuisance. I need the reassurance. I need somebody strong to keep them away. Can you do that? They're so pesky. They bother me all the time. I need them. If they knew where I am, they'd be calling."

"The phone's turned off."

"Oh no! So that's what that little buzzing was, like a far-off fly! The phone has to be on. It has to be answered. Don't you want to know who's calling?"

"No," Marnie says, but she turns the phone back on.

I say, "Turning it off doesn't achieve anything. What's necessary is to make them *afraid* to call. Can you make them afraid?"

"Sure."

"Even Elise?"

"Especially Elise."

"No you couldn't. You're too nice. You may be a bear, but it's a Teddy bear. You're a creampuff. I could fall into you like a cloud. I could disappear. I could become a corpuscle in your blood and wander inside you forever. Elise gave me gold. She flaunted me in my gold like First Prize. Why can't I have a lover like you?"

"You can."

"And we can doze like this with our noses in each other's ears, like chihuahuas, and you won't say, 'I didn't join the automatic criminal class and break my mother's heart and deny myself a house in Westchester and money and power and fame and children and immortality, to doze in somebody's ear.' Will you?"

"Hardly ever."

"All right then. In three years. When you're older and ready to settle down. Let's go buy the *Times*."

At first our bodies will not part, but we promise them they'll be joined again in twenty minutes, and after many failures and sighs, much trembling and coming, they do part. Oh, it's wonderful to have

chain-reaction comes without working at them, like a
sky full of electricity randomly dropping lightning,
and pretend they're a bother, and laugh, and not be
tragic — though I do force myself into a butch
thought: Is it always like this for Marnie? I try to
flare my nostrils, just for the practice. I can't. I try
to say, "Do you do this with everybody?" I can't, any
more than I could ask Artemis or Demeter to
explain herself.

Marnie is not a femme after all, or a butch
either. She is a *dyke*. She is as strong as possible.

Is the infamous Nadine a dyke too? I'll think
about that tomorrow.

We dress and walk on wobbly legs to the
newsstand at Sheridan Square. There's a crowd
hunched in the nippy wind waiting for the papers.
Without my glasses, I never know when I'm gazing
at someone. I wish my eyes didn't seal shut at the
thought of contact lenses. Myopia may be pretty, but
it does get me into trouble.

And here's proof again, a dim looming Thing
saying, "Hi to you too, Baby," while I smile vaguely
in case he's someone I know. This happens every
time I go out without my glasses. I really must do
something about my vanity and wear the damn ugly
things.

Marnie asks, "Do you know this man?"

"No," I say. (I probably don't.)

Marnie, making herself huge the way a cat
makes itself heavy, says, "Then why don't you shove
off, Buddy?"

"Buddy!" he says. "Big butch *Buddy*. What are
you doing with her, a beautiful girl like her?"

If I wear my glasses, who's going to call me beautiful?

Marnie tells him, "Go!" and I think oh God, he'll pull a knife, he'll pull a broken bottle, but he goes, yelling, "So long, *Buddy*! Have fun, *Buddy*!"

I'm quite impressed. Elise would have threatened him with Mace, but Marnie threatened him with an Olympian thunderbolt.

I think it's all spoiled now, all that sweet sexy peaceful drifty wobbly feeling all gone. Marnie's full of adrenalin, I'm full of remorse for being insane and vain, wanting the plaudits of the masses, willing to sacrifice fifty acres of trees for the crossword puzzle. (I never look at the rest of the paper.)

And Marnie hands me this huge inky mass because she sees a board, "a perfect shelf board" she calls it, leaning against a garbage can. Before I can stop her, she has *touched* it, she is picking it up. "No!" I cry. "It's got leprosy. It's got botulism. I'll *buy* you a board." She laughs and leaves it, but she's dirty now.

I dig in her pocket for her key. "Keep your mitts off this key," I say. We climb the stairs to her little cheap dingy cell. I unlock the door. She heads at once for the bathroom, but I get there first, to keep her hands off the faucet. I start the water. "Wash!" I say, and she washes, saying she does hope I know she would have anyway. I wonder if I do know. I wonder where she got the rest of her shelves.

And now I really know everything's spoiled, because I have become my mother, and Marnie has become Elise's mother, Elise's poor heavy tragic

babushka mother. "Who is that *woman?*" my mother
asked after they met, not supposing my elegant rich
stockbroker Elise could come from that, because
blood does tell, even in America. "Who is this
woman?" I am thinking. "Who is this fat woman?"

Marnie loves to watch me remove my makeup,
just as Elise's mother did. I had no other way to
entertain Elise's mother. Like her, Marnie just
watches, doesn't touch. Sits on the bathtub rim and
watches. I become White Mouse. Doesn't she notice?
Why that look of sappy pleasure if she notices? Only
rewinding the film, turning White Mouse back into
Looker, Knockout, Wow, made Elise's mother
happier.

Why can't the infamous Nadine cure me of
wanting everybody to love me?

I say, "Elise's mother is so gloomy, so depressed,
and one time I heard her humming and I was so
pleased, but then I listened closer. She was
humming 'The Volga Boatman.'"

Marnie's laugh brings the Elf back. Thank God. I
hate being my mother.

Marnie is perfectly clean already. What is she
doing in the shower? Why is she brushing her teeth?
I've opened the couch into a pure white bed in this
pure white room that smells of sweet woodruff and
chamomile, and she's still gurgling in there like a
whale. If these walls weren't so thin I'd yell, "Hurry
up! I'm cold!"

Here she is, naked, lovely masses, warm, but the
honeymoon is over. We fall asleep as comfy-cozy as
Mr. and Mrs. Miniver. The next big event will be

the Golden Wedding, I think, but next morning once again we can't get apart, and the puzzle goes undone.

I think this is what freedom is for, living by my own morals instead of Elise's. It is so incredibly refreshing, it's so much fun, but I'm afraid I overdo it. I take home three women in three nights, and it's not really fun because they're something like Elise, plotting to cage me, and anyway my health isn't equal to such exertions. Marnie was the only fun one — but as the infamous Nadine says, someday one really must grow up, give up insanity, keep one's word, become one single person who can promise. It may be bliss to be a corpuscle in Marnie's blood, but it can't be called adult.

I dream I'm in a hospital bed. Standing on my right is Nadine, on my left Marnie. I'm supposed to choose between them, but I wake up instead of choosing.

Nadine will be pleased when I tell her she was on the right.

Marnie doesn't require enough. She wouldn't care if I never grew up.

"Lynn? It's Marnie. I've got long lines of wailing women at my door, saying you've gone back to Elise. Have you?"

"Oh, Marnie, I'm sorry. I really had to. Don't you think so? I hope I haven't hurt you."

"No. The opposite. I was on the verge of feeling like a loser, and here you suddenly were, and now I doubt I'll ever feel like a loser."

"Thank you, thank you, Marnie," I say. "Every other person I ever went to bed with screams at me, 'You bitch, you ruined my life!' "

"Well, not mine. I have fulfilled the ambition of every man, woman, and child in the United States," dear Marnie says. "I have made love with Ingrid Bergman."

Marnie can allow herself these unrealities because she's not crazy.

"It never occurred to me I could keep her," she says.

Music Video

Elisabeth Nonas

Just in time," my office manager greets me as I
come back from lunch. "We got an emergency — has
to be out by tomorrow."

I fill a glass with water from the cooler. "Amalia,
it's too hot to rush." Los Angeles is having a heat
wave. Buildings shimmer in the magic of the hot air.
I'm wearing a sleeveless T-shirt and light cotton
shorts but even these seem to weigh me down. I
look forward to getting back to my dim editing room.
"Who's the rush?"

"The new Tamara single."

Tamara is as big a star as Madonna, Janet Jackson, Paula Abdul. Her videos become media events.

"Oh no," I say. "You know my policy."

"Diane, there's no one else."

"Amalia. No."

"Clock's ticking boss, client's waiting."

I argue. "Jess is not a client."

"Today she is."

I stalk down the hall. I'm five years old, whiny. I own this company, I shouldn't have to take projects I don't want. I turn back to Amalia's desk. "Where's everyone else?"

"Booked." Amalia stares me down. I hired her because she isn't afraid of me. Today I regret this. Amalia swings her arm out, finger pointed down the hallway. I'm ten now, obedient but reluctant.

Jess sits with her back to the door. Her arms are raised, fingers linked together behind her head holding her wavy dark hair off her neck. Short sleeves of her shirt rolled over her nicely shaped biceps, an inch or two of bangle bracelets on her right arm, sports watch on her left. She leans back in the big leather chair, one foot anchored on the ground gently swinging the chair side to side. She's wearing khaki shorts and deck shoes. Her other leg — great calf muscle — is draped over the arm of the chair.

I can smell her perfume.

I clear my throat. "Want anything before we start — coffee, water, soda?"

"Diane, this wasn't my idea." She faces me.

How eyes that light got matched with hair that dark is a marvel to me.

"We were scheduled for tomorrow with Carla but MTV moved up the air date ..." She trails off, giving me a softly apologetic look. She lowers her arms. Dark tumbles around her face, her bright eyes shine.

"Maybe this time it'll be different," I mutter, settling in at the console.

Jess and I have been a couple for ten years and lived together for nine. She produces and sometimes directs music videos. I edit videos. She cuts most of hers at my shop, and I love dropping in on a session, or knowing that she's down the hall while I'm busy with something else. When she's around we sometimes have lunch together, or drive in to work together, and it's fun. But my policy is not to cut with Jess. We're extremely compatible in many ways, and that's what makes our relationship work so well after all these years. We can each tolerate about the same amount of mess around the house, we both like to get up early. Our schedules are busy but we make time for each other and it's been fine so far.

I believe that's because we don't work together. We tried it once, years ago when Jess first started in music videos. A disaster. We didn't talk for two weeks afterward. We each have very strong opinions on how something should look. And I had lots more experience with editing. Jess had good ideas, but she wouldn't listen to any of my suggestions. Then she pulled rank on me — reminding me the client is always right.

Maybe it's something we should have worked

through differently so that we could edit together but I like the way we resolved it. I've had the best of both worlds until this moment when I'm sitting next to the love of my life who is now my client. I am not looking forward to this session.

"Let's see what we've got." I slide a cassette into the machine.

The image on the monitor shows Tamara in a tight close-up. "Is the whole thing in black and white?" I ask.

Jess nods. "This is for the story line that we'll be intercutting with Tamara at her recording session. That part's in color."

The song is called *(You've Always Been) My Best Friend.* Tamara's voice is full and deep. She's known as a real belter. But this song is a little slower than her usual, softer, with a real sexy bass riff. I only half listen to the lyrics. I play the music randomly. I want to get a sense of how the images will go with it.

The video has the feel of an old Italian movie. Maybe it's the black and white, or Tamara's looks — she's a cross between a young Sophia Loren and Gabriella Sabatini, the tennis player — sort of sultry and athletic at the same time, which makes sense, since Tamara trained as a dancer.

I adjust the volume as the camera pulls back to reveal Tamara lying on a beach blanket. Her body glistens. She's wearing a white string bikini, the kind they just banned in Palm Springs, California. "Holy cow," I murmur.

"It gets better," Jess says.

Tamara stretches slowly. The muscles on her arms tighten. "Has she been working out?" I ask. "Great definition." I can't look as long as I'd like because the camera slides off Tamara's shoulders to her breasts, which appear small, the nipples erect. I could count each of her ribs if the camera weren't drawing me down her body. Her stomach is so flat her hip bones cause a gap in her suit. I myself couldn't caress her thighs as well as the camera is doing. Her quadriceps are sleek, her calf muscles almost as good as Jess's.

"Will MTV run this?" I ask.

"Wait," is all Jess says.

The camera finishes its loving exploration of Tamara's legs and feet and Tamara slowly turns onto her stomach.

I let out an involuntary gasp. "No wonder they want to ban those things." The bottom of Tamara's bikini has no back, only a string that runs from between her legs to meet the string that circles her waist. Her ass is perfectly smooth and round, the most lovely invitation I've seen in years. Her waist dips daintily in, flares out again in perfect proportion to her fine back and strong shoulders.

The screen flicks to black. End of that take. I wipe my forehead. "Is the air not on in here or is it just the video?"

"Wait," says Jess.

We sit through three more takes like the first. We're watching these dailies because I'm supposed to be paying attention to what I want to use in the rough cut, but all I can see is smooth skin and that round, round ass.

In the next scene Tamara is sitting up, smoothing suntan oil on her arms, chest, and legs. Her body gleams. In all, four takes of that.

The camera watches Tamara like a lover. I glance over at Jess. Eyes intent on the monitor, fingers of her right hand absently stroking her bare thigh.

I can hear myself swallow. Like when you're about to kiss someone for the first time but neither of you know who's going to make the next move.

Next scene, new set-up, a little further away revealing more of the beach. A deserted stretch of sand, rocky cliffs in the distance. Tamara still sitting up on her blanket, but we see now that she's not alone. Another woman is lying on a blanket a few feet away from her. They've come equipped for a day's outing. Picnic basket, boom box, umbrella, frisbee.

The other woman is lying on her back with her eyes closed. She's just come out of the ocean, water beads over her trim body. Her boyishly cut black hair is wet, too, off her face, like she's just run her hands through it. She looks French maybe, or Italian. Her string bikini is black.

Tamara is finishing with the oil on her arms. Now, new action, she stretches to put some on her back. But she can't reach everywhere. She looks at her friend, leans over and nudges her, holding out the oil. The friend looks up, one hand shading her eyes. Tamara hands her the tube of oil.

Three takes of this. The friend isn't as classically beautiful as Tamara, but she'd stop traffic on the street. She has an androgynous look and pouty lips, the darkest eyes. Make-believe tough — might be the kind whose first kisses are playful little bites.

Next scene. Medium shot. Tamara is on her stomach, arms at her side. Her friend enters the frame, holding the tube of oil. She squeezes out the shape of a heart on Tamara's back, studies it a moment, then begins to smooth the oil across Tamara's skin. She unhooks the tiny bra strap, applies more oil, lays down the tube, and begins rubbing with both hands now. Around the shoulder blades, along the spine, dangerously close to that roundest of invitations, always returning up again, then sliding down.

My skin is electric. Jess isn't saying anything, but I hear her breathing — or imagine I can — and the music of her bracelets when she lifts her hair off her neck.

The woman leans over and whispers something in Tamara's ear. Tamara smiles, her eyes still closed. The woman smiles. Whispers something else. Tamara raises her torso off the blanket. The top of her bikini slips off as she slides onto her back.

"Jesus god," I whisper.

Tamara's breasts aren't so small after all. And her nipples are perfect dark berries.

Jess lays her left hand on my thigh, just under the cuff of my shorts.

"We can't use this for TV," I say.

"Then let's use it now," says Jess. She spreads

her hand on my thigh. Her little finger grazes the elastic of my briefs.

"Cut it out," I whisper. "The door's not closed all the way."

"Shh," Jess says, pulling my chair closer and leaning forward to kiss me.

Jess is the only woman I've kissed for the last ten years. The only one I've made love with in that time. And yet. It's the and yet that keeps us together. The and yet that makes her so familiar and still a stranger, exotic and unknown — still the other, always my Jess.

So this kiss is familiar and yet. Today the and yet is the open door to the edit room. I hear Amalia talking to clients. The and yet is I'm the owner of this company, four other edit bays in use at this very moment, and my lover is climbing onto my chair, straddling my thighs while I fumble at the buttons on her shirt, managing to open three out of four before I yank it off her shoulders. It hangs around her waist.

Jess's lips leave mine, travel down my neck. On screen Tamara wets her lips. At the bottom of the monitors numbers spin faster than my eyes can register them, counting frames and running time.

The camera caresses Tamara's smooth shoulder as I tongue my way down Jess's side. In extreme close-up Tamara's friend digs her fingers into Tamara's back as Jess kneads mine and I suck at her breast. Tamara's song plays. Our hands move against the rhythm but our hips strain together in time. I'm watching the monitors. I see hips or thighs or stomachs — abstract dune shapes impossible to decipher until Tamara moves or I close my eyes because Jess has found her way into my shorts and inside me. "You're so wet," she whispers against my ear, giving me chills.

I urgently undo the buttons on her shorts. Again, not all, just enough to give me access to her smooth hips, from there gliding around to her ass so I can reach between her legs. I slide a finger from each hand inside her. She moans. I pull out of her — "No," she whispers — to enter from the front, again a finger from each hand, palms up, an offering. She sits back against my hands.

This is trust. We're balanced here on my chair, both leaning back — Jess to keep me inside her, me to support our weight in this tricky position. Our faces are two feet from each other. I watch my lover. Her mouth is open, eyes closed, head tilted slightly to the side as if listening for something far away. But I know what she's hearing because it's building in me as well and I press deeper inside her. I move my thumbs on her clitoris. Jess opens her eyes — they're so clear that some trick of perception enables me to see through them, I think, deeper than should be possible.

On the monitor Tamara and her friend continue to repeat gestures and actions — a smile, a wink, a caress — but now I'm watching Jess. I do not move at all. My hands are still, I brace them for Jess, who uses them as she will, grinding and writhing. My muscles are beginning to tremble with the strain. Perspiration rolls off my face, off Jess's body. All the heat of the day has gathered inside Jess, where my fingers meet.

Not just the heat but all the stillness has moved into her as well. She balances on her knees and against my arms, hands on the arms of my chair, hovering on the edge of an expectant tension. She looks at me still.

Her release begins slowly, visible first as a clouding of her eyes, still open but unseeing. Her mouth open too, but inarticulate. Softest exhalation "Ohh." Still soft, but no less powerful "Ohhhh" this time, longer as she thrusts hard against my hands, my arms — all hers now as she raises herself so that I think she's finished but no, comes back down, and down again, then leans back all the way, pushing harder, all my strength to hold her on my lap — "Yes yes yes oh god yes" — as she shudders then is still.

All is still — the heat returned to the room, to the air, holding everything in place. My arms wet with sweat, mine and Jess's. I am still inside her. Her pulse beats around my fingers.

Jess leans to kiss me and my fingers slip out of her. I run my hands along her back, over her shoulders, down her arms. Her skin is glazed with moisture. I pull her shirt back over her shoulders but do not button it. She takes my hand, kisses the palm, lays it over her breast. Her breathing has not yet returned to normal. She leans forward, tongues my ear. "Now you."

"Can't. I'm working."

"Who's the client?" she asks.

I try to protest but she silences me with her lips and tongue. Whispers against my ear "The client's always right," climbs off me, sits back in her chair. "Now," she says, "re-rack the tape back to the first shot where we see her ass. Good. Now," she says patting her thighs, "come here."

I think, We shouldn't be doing this. I think, What if someone walks in, this could be trouble, we were just lucky this time.

"Come on," Jess says again, urgent now.

I think, And yet.

I go willingly.

Making History

Robbi Sommers

Cass took a last drag off her cigarette and exhaled slowly. As the bell tower chimed, a wave of inertia swept through her. Late for world history class and she didn't care. Cass dropped the cigarette butt to the ground and crushed it beneath her black boot. To be prisoner in a small classroom, victim to Professor Calloway's insipid droning, seemed a dim alternative when spring so blatantly beckoned her to climb on her bike and ride to the coast.

Cass leaned against the building's stone wall and

watched the last stragglers climb the steps to the dark windowless doors. How world history was going to improve her auto mechanic skills, she couldn't figure.

"I don't think so," she said aloud. She shook her head and reached into her leather jacket for her keys. Mariette, Cass's most recent ex-lover, had insisted that Cass give college a chance.

"After all," Mariette had nagged on many occasions, "you'll go farther in business these days with a degree."

"I don't think so," Cass repeated as she climbed onto her Harley and sliced the key into the ignition. Two weeks of higher education and she had had enough.

"Aren't you coming to class?" A woman's voice broke into Cass's thoughts.

Cass glanced over her shoulder to see Ms. Lipson, Professor Calloway's assistant. With a tentative smile, one that projected an alluring innocence, Ms. Lipson moved closer to the front of the bike.

Her dark hair was a deluge of wild curls whisked haphazardly from her face by a golden barrette. A losing attempt at control, Cass thought, amused. She hadn't paid much attention to the Professor's assistant while daydreaming in class. But out of that stifling classroom, taking a moment to appreciate things from a freer perspective, Cass was quite attracted to the freckle-faced assistant.

"I don't think so, Ms. Lipson." Cass let the words slide out slowly, placing added emphasis on the syllables of Ms. Lipson's name. "Gonna do some research work, out in the field, so to speak."

"It's just that today's somewhat important," Ms. Lipson said as she appraised her reflection in Cass's mirrored sunglasses. "Professor Calloway's going to announce —"

"Gonna cruise the coast," Cass interrupted. "Beautiful day, kind of day for making history, know what I mean?" Her words sparkled suggestively.

Seemingly brushing aside the innuendo, Ms. Lipson glanced briefly at the large clock on the bell tower. "Got to run," she said although her voice lacked conviction. She turned toward the building.

Cass impulsively grabbed the back of Ms. Lipson's full skirt.

"What if you missed the day? One lousy day? What if you climbed on my bike and rode with me to the ocean? One lousy day, for history's sake." Cass realized that grabbing Ms. Lipson's skirt was brazen, her suggestion reckless. But occasionally, on instinct, Cass spontaneously shot from the hip. A butch prerogative, she supposed.

Ms. Lipson turned to Cass, who had not let go of the skirt that now twisted close around her body. The sight of her floral skirt, tightly grasped in Cass's thick fingers, sent a sudden excitement through her.

Not a surprise, she thought as her eyes focused on the strong hand, drifted up the leather jacket, scanned the silver zippers, the raised collar, the mirrored eyes, and then fixed on Cass's spiked black hair. No, not a surprise at all.

She had noticed Cass from the first day of class. With her leather jacket and her thick, steel-toed black boots, the woman was always a few minutes late, slipping into a back seat as if no one would notice, as if no one cared.

But Leanna, better known as the aspiring Ms. Lipson, had noticed. The woman's subtle smirk, her cool attitude — never took her sunglasses off, never removed her jacket — Leanna had noticed all right. Five-foot-seven, Leanna had guessed, although the boots had a high square heel, maybe five-six. A strong build, the woman looked tough, with a solid ass, Leanna had noted more than once, that was curved and sweetly emphasized in her tight jeans.

"One lousy day?" Leanna said as though engaged in contemplative debate.

"For history's sake," Cass offered.

As the woman spoke, Leanna wondered about her eyes, still hidden behind the mirrored lenses. She imagined them deep ebony.

"I'm Leanna," she said meaning yes, okay, for history's sake.

"Cass," Cass replied knowing exactly what Leanna meant. She lifted the glasses slightly from her charcoal eyes.

Yes, Leanna was right. They were dark, like coals, and they burned right through her. That kind of eyes, oh yes, Leanna had known all along.

Cass, realizing she still had a handful of Leanna's skirt, let the material fall. The wrinkle in the fabric left a lingering mark where Cass had grasped, apparently tighter than she had thought.

Leanna ran her hand over the wrinkle then

looked back at Cass, who had dropped the glasses back over her eyes.

"Delicate material," Leanna murmured, as though clarifying her nature rather than discussing the fabric.

"So I see," Cass said in a low voice. God, she loved femme women. "So I see."

As they rode along the coast, the salt-laden breeze lashed across Cass's cheeks, whipped through her hair. The ocean air filled her with an unbridled sense of freedom. She scanned the vast ocean, the heated sand. With Leanna's arms wrapped tightly around her waist, her face pressed close to Cass's neck, it was difficult to restrain the frolicking fantasies of a seaside affair.

How she had sat in that class for two weeks and never zeroed in on Leanna was beyond her comprehension. A stone butch, a solid butch, she ritually noticed, sized up and then extended every femme a fair chance. Obviously, her splash into higher education, so against her nature, had made her carelessly indifferent to her surroundings. Uncharacteristically, she had overlooked this luscious woman.

Cass headed toward the cove, her cove, the secluded spot she had found once, months ago, on a solo exploration of the coast. Here she would take Leanna. They could sit in the sun, listen to the ocean's heart beat — hold hands, take off their tops, embrace as their sun-kissed breasts touched.

Cass had the scenario complete as she pulled her bike to the side of the dirt road. She would take Leanna's hand, lead her past the thick brush laden with purple wildflowers, up and over the sun-bleached sand dunes and around the bend to the private cove.

As she climbed from her bike, Cass imagined unhinging the barrette, tangling her fingers through Leanna's unleashed curls. Her hands felt suddenly heated. On the beach, she would press her hands against Leanna's unrestrained breasts, glide her fingers in the soft curls hidden beneath the floral skirt.

"I know a place," Cass said as she helped Leanna off the bike, "not too far down the path." She took Leanna's hand and led her past the wine-purple flowers.

"My shoes," Leanna said as she headed for a large boulder on the side of the path.

As Leanna unlaced her sandals, Cass watched her flowered skirt flirtatiously lift above her thigh. A glimpse of pink lace, a flash of tanned flesh, teased Cass unmercifully. Cass sighed silently. A hot hunger simmered deep within.

"The ride was wonderful!" Leanna said climbing off the rock. "I haven't been out to the coast since last summer." Her vibrant smile lit her entire face. "And your bike is so —!"

"You don't regret missing history, do you?" Cass laughed, attempting to take Leanna's hand.

"We're making history, remember?" Leanna said with an unexpected bold edge to her voice. She reached her arm around Cass and pulled her in close.

When they reached the dunes, Cass slipped, as though inadvertently, from Leanna's hold. Having put her arm around Cass as if she had no concept of who was the butch, who was in charge, Leanna's aggressiveness had unsettled Cass.

"C'mere you," Cass said as she grabbed Leanna's hand, this time making sure to connect. She broke into a run up the dunes.

Leanna, holding on tight, ran behind Cass. The hot sand felt good against her bare feet. She jumped, leaped as they ran. Shouting with childlike glee, she laughed with delight as they came down the dunes, rounded the bend and tumbled into the deserted cove.

As they rolled in the sand, Leanna reflected on her two-week crush on Cass. She had wanted Cass from day one. When Leanna wanted something, Leanna got it. That's just the way things went. Had she known that today was going to be the day, perhaps she would have dressed more appropriately. Her pink panties would not have been her first choice. She would have worn black. She would have run a trail of perfume into her secret hair. She would have —

Cass rolled above Leanna and began smothering her with desperate kisses. The rough sand invaded Leanna's tank top, pressed into Leanna's delicate skin. If Leanna had known today was the day, she would have worn leather, would have worn lace, her silver-toed black boots. She would have tied her hair tight from her face, painted her lips in scarlet reds, smudged her eyelids with shadowy grays. If she had known —

Cass felt deliriously aroused. Leanna was so soft,

so vulnerable. She was every butch's dream. Pulling the barrette from Leanna's hair, Cass grabbed into the curls, smothering herself in the perfumed silkiness.

Cass was climbing, oh yes. The passion intensifying. She pulled at Leanna's top, ripped at it, lifted it to expose her pink lace bra. So very femme, Cass thought hungrily, so open to surrender. She pulled the lace cup aside and her mouth fastened onto Leanna's hardening nipple.

Leanna moaned. As her nipple stiffened, she felt red heat shoot through to her clit. She was swelling, she could feel it. Her heartbeat throbbed in her creaming flesh. Her slit involuntarily opened and contracted with each tight suck on her electric nipple.

Leanna tried to shove her hand into Cass's jeans. She wanted to wallow in secretions, smear Cass's sap anywhere she could. But Cass grabbed her hand and pushed it aside with a typical stone butch "I do you and that's it" demeanor.

Leanna knew this type of butch woman. This was her specialty. If she could get Cass's pants off, the rest would be simple. She loved a challenge. The anticipation, the mystery of not knowing and then the final surrender made her crazy with desire.

Laughing, Leanna pushed from under Cass and headed toward the water. She cast her clothes aside as she ran.

"C'mon, come get me," she teased.

Leanna circled and splashed at the water's edge. Unbearably aroused, Cass watched Leanna's small round breasts as she danced. The nipples seemed to strain from the dark pink areolas. As Leanna swirled, her breasts taunted and her ripe ass teased.

"Come get me!" Leanna called again and she rushed into an incoming low wave.

Cass licked her dry lips. Quick visions of lying on Leanna, fucking her as the waves rolled over them both soared through her mind. The fantasy was too much to contain. Cass tossed her jacket aside, ripped off her shirt, climbed out of her jeans and ran to Leanna.

Leanna, drenched from the wave, turned just in time to see Cass reach the water. Leanna's heart beat quickened.

"Her pants are off," she whispered, exhilarated.

Cass splashed into the water and grabbed Leanna. They fell to the wet sand and the warm ocean caressed their naked bodies. Breasts pressing breasts, rock-flesh nipples extended, Cass rubbed against Leanna, Leanna glided against Cass.

The water squished between them, pulled away, came again. Cass slid her eager tongue between Leanna's salt-laced lips. She tangled her legs in Leanna's and together, kissing, exploring the heat of their mouths, they rolled along the wet bed of the ocean's edge.

Leanna was hot, yet she was patient. She slid against Cass, rolled with Cass, let Cass rush her hands up her body, in her hair, over her breasts, between her legs. Cass was letting go, wallowing in Leanna's pleasures.

In a quick moment, as they rolled again, Leanna

made her move. Cass had overturned, her belly flat
against the sand. Leanna pressed her full pussy
against the muscular arch of Cass's tight ass.

"Move your ass for me," Leanna pleaded, her
mouth only inches from Cass's ear.

Uneasy, Cass tried to move from beneath Leanna.
No way she'd bottom for some suddenly out of
bounds, pseudo-top femme.

"Please don't," Leanna begged in a sweet, sweet
tone. "If you'd rock your ass for me, a special way, I
can come so hard."

And what true butch wouldn't help a lady, Cass
thought, not aware that Leanna knew this fact all
too well.

"Just want me to rock my ass, huh?" Cass asked,
her voice low, laden with butch attitude.

What harm, Cass thought, would just moving her
ass be. A provocative smile crossed Cass's face. She'd
play along, see what got this little lady off.

Leanna straddled Cass's ass. Slowly she lowered
her pussy toward the cleft between Cass's tight
cheeks. When Leanna spread her legs, the lips of
her pussy naturally sliced open. She had that kind
of pussy, one that her previous lovers had said was
"made to be fucked." "So thick," "so pulpy," "so
meaty," "so lush"; those were the kinds of words
women had whispered, cried, exclaimed when they
saw her fleshy pussy, her large clitoris.

Leanna was wet, so wet that drops of white had
dripped from her opening onto Cass's ass and
dribbled into the crack. With both hands, Leanna
spread the thick mounds of flesh and pressed her
quivering clit wedge into the slit.

"Tighten your ass." Her words were soft, feminine, non-threatening.

The water lapped between their bodies, pulled away, in constant rhythm. Repeatedly, the water rushed, surrounded, let go.

Cass was astonished that she could feel Leanna's erect clitoral flesh between her cheeks. How large, how incredibly pronounced Leanna's sex was. Rigid, almost rubberlike in texture, the over-endowed clit seemed to force its way between her buttocks.

As Leanna had so sweetly asked, Cass tightened down and felt her ass enfold the pulpy clit. Keeping a tight grip, Cass slowly rocked her ass as she tugged the chunky sex organ.

"That's it," Leanna coaxed. "Pump me off, baby."

Sex was dripping from Leanna's pearl pudding pussy. The ocean washed the milkwater away, only to be defeated by the unending secretion's return.

Leanna was crazy hot. She plucked and squeezed her own nipples as she urged Cass to tighten then release her meaty ass.

Cass willingly obliged. She continued to clip the dangling, distended clit between the bulky halves of her butt.

"Got you baby, got you good, don't I baby?" Cass's words were gruff, demanding, like the increased pressing of her ass muscles.

Leanna tried to pull back, but her clit was held fast between the cheeks. As she lifted, her clit seemed to stretch tight. She bounced lightly, watching the tensing ass that held her blood red clit hostage.

A devastatingly intoxicating sensation jammed

through her and Leanna's ascent reached a peak. She was there, she was there.

"Clip it baby, clamp it baby!" Leanna cried out in pleasure.

Cass tensed her ass tighter than she dreamed possible and rocked, bucked, took the femme for the ride of her life.

"Got you now, got you now!" Cass said blindly, out of sorts herself.

As Leanna cranked off, she reached beneath Cass's rocking ass and slammed her fingers deep into Cass's water-caressed cunt. The action caught Cass off guard. She tried to pull away, causing her legs to open and Leanna's fingers to have better access.

"Oh god!" Cass shouted. She wanted Leanna to stop, she was stone butch, there was no room for this sort of sex. And yet, those fingers, diving, prying, tunneling were creating an unrivaled sensation.

Cass clamped down. This had to stop, she was losing control. Yet the clamping only made the thrusting feel better.

"I'll stop if you want," Leanna, on top, whispered in a rush of heated words. She was on the verge of another orgasm just from watching Cass's pleasure.

"No, yes, no, yes, no, yes," Cass screamed as she crashed into the hardest come she had ever experienced.

For Leanna — looked femme, fucked butch — penetrating a stone butch, watching her cross over, was the ultimate. As she thrust into Cass's barely trespassed slit, Leanna creamed into a spectacular orgasm, collapsing simultaneously with Cass. And the restless waves continued to lick at their throbbing pussies as if the sea partook in their pleasure.

Slightly shifting, Leanna ran her fingers through Cass's wet hair. "Any regrets?" She murmured. She hoped that she hadn't pushed too far, too fast, with Cass.

Cass rolled from beneath Leanna. She hesitated for a moment, then sat up. Running her hand through her spiked hair, she then cocked her head with typical butch attitude.

Cass peered out to the restless ocean, then shifted her attention to Leanna. Without a word, she looked intently at Leanna, as though appraising her for the first time. Leanna, still unsure, rested her hand lightly on Cass's.

Subtly, like a tender bud sprouting from broken concrete, a soft smile began to blossom from Cass's stone butch lips.

"My only regret," she said turning her gaze again to the ocean. "Is the history I've missed."

Going Up

Dorothy Tell

I woke from raggedy sleep, my hair moist and crumpled against the pillow. I lay still, on my back, willing my hands to remain calm and flat on the sheets beside my upper thighs.

The event of the past week and its unexpected, unsettling outcome was still fresh behind my eyes, running through my mind like a movie I could not turn off. Where had I gone wrong? Had I not done everything? Followed all the rules for success? And how had my discipline served me? I ticked off the bleak facts of my life.

Alone at forty-two, a career woman — full director since last Tuesday — a woman now failed by the once glowing idea that mere achievement of goals brings happiness. A woman with no lovers, no children, no pets. *Nothing* to turn focus from that climb up the corporate stairs. I had kept my body in top physical shape, dressed properly, with the correct amount of aggression and color. I had cheerfully taken all the worst travel assignments, re-invested my bonuses in company stock. I had slept with the men who would help me, my eyes always on the prize of power and attainment of personal goals.

And now, after all the hard-driving years, why did this pall of emptiness invade my life? My mind cast about for balm and found none. I had believed the great lie, that once at the top there were no problems money and power could not solve. With a sharp sting of epiphany I realized I had broken the glass ceiling and found nothing there except more of the games men deemed important. Resentment boiled within as chagrin replaced despair.

Then with no seeming connection, images of the two women at work filled my mind and my heartbeat quickened.

I told myself to be calm, that this morning would be different. After all, a trained, controlled, corporate warrior should be able to hold her emotions in check ... should not continue to succumb to the unhealthy obsession with what two other women were doing every morning in the elevator at work.

And they were doing something. Of that I was sure.

All my self-talk was to no avail. I remembered the tall one's smile, the crooked lift to her curving upper lip and the challenge in her eyes. An insistent pulsing began between my legs. My hands moved over my hips and downward toward the twitching center of my shame, fingers slipping into the wetness, pulling, stroking, pinching my hardened clitoris.

The vision grew in my mind, a magnified close-up in my memory of the tall woman's long fingers caressing the small woman's hip, then sliding out of sight under her short jacket. My physical urgency became desperate and I could not stroke myself fast enough, hard enough.

I flopped onto my belly and bunched the pillow beneath me, humping and slapping my spread vagina down against the knuckles of my fisted hand. Release eluded me. I remained suspended at that electric, painful point of almost there.

I squeezed my eyes tight and remembered the way the two women had moved against each other, one in front, one in back — both facing the door as the elevator slowly rose past twenty-nine floors. How they had pressed closer to the back wall as people got on and off at each stop. And how the tall one's eyes had found mine as I stood beside them with my mouth agape, trying not to breathe.

The memory of her smiling eyes impacted immediately upon my suspended sexual release. I extended my fingers and felt the shaft and head of my clitoris grow hard. I turned onto my back. The pillow, now beneath my bottom, thrust my pelvis upward. I clamped my legs tightly together and drove my middle finger onto and past my clitoris. I flicked the nipples of both breasts with my free hand, tending one, then the other, kneading and pinching as my urgency grew.

My lower body leaped to meet my fingers, surging toward orgasm. My pressed lips held back sound as I pounded again and again upon that throbbing nub where all feeling gathered.

Afterward, I lay still, my heart leaping in my chest, as surges of orgasmic pleasure rolled from my swollen vagina outward, down my legs, along my spread arms.

But full release would not come.

My mind's eye focused again on the opiate image of smiling lips and of a woman's eyes sparkling with the knowledge of a forbidden joy. Recalling those teasing eyes worked a bittersweet magic on my beleaguered clitoris and it thrilled again, hardened and aching as I left my bed and walked to the shower.

I washed my body thoroughly, rubbing my skin hard, as if I could somehow scrub away the effects of what I had come almost to cherish as my own peculiar torment ... the tortured need to share the illicit excitement of the women in the elevator.

I inspected my face in the bathroom mirror. The planes were still good, the angles strong, chin firm, eyes steady. I twisted my hair and pinned it back, turning to survey the curve of my neck. A neck every bit as nice as the tall one's neck. I looked down at my breasts. The tips were dark and ripe. I tore my gaze away and looked again into the mirror. No sign of my obsession was visible on my countenance, but even as my lips in the mirror

rounded over the *no!* in my brain, my body rebelled
and the pulsing began anew in my groin.

My heart quickened and a sinking knowledge
filled me. I knew I had to do it, that I could not
resist the shameful activity which had become a
heated compulsion. I knew I must stand again beside
those women and experience the excitement I craved
like a drug.

I arrived at work my usual quarter hour early so
I could appear to browse magazines at the
concessionaire's nook by the lobby elevator while I
waited for the two women to appear.

I was barely conscious of the others who moved
purposefully about the lobby making their way to the
maze of offices that rose like stacks of children's
blocks above us. My only focus was upon the
excitement which I knew would soon come.

My hands trembled as I flipped unseen pages. A
rush of urgency unfolded deep within me. My mouth
was dry and a tiny rivulet of perspiration gathered
in the crevice of my buttocks, adding its annoying
tickle to the growing agitation in my vagina. Each
time I looked up to search for the women, expectant
thrills of excitement shot down my legs. My
obsession controlled me.

I was on the verge of tears. I wanted to shout, to
cry, to hurt myself. To flail my arms against this
incomprehensible need ... pound my fist against my
clamoring clitoris.

I wanted to *be* those women.

To embrace them.

To come between them.

A burst of light filled my brain as the thought

became an image of such power that I clutched the counter edge to keep from sinking to my knees.

To come between them.

My hardened clitoris pulsed as raw need transported me. If the women did not soon appear, I would have to slip into the women's room and relieve the heated ache between my legs.

My despair turned to fluttering joy as I caught sight of the tall one striding through the doors and with easy confidence across the marble floor toward the elevators. I felt each hard click of her high heels as she came closer. I memorized the lines and curves of her body as those sharp heels tapped the shiny floor. Her lemon-colored hair bounced and swung as her hips rolled forward for each step.

I waited, spellbound as usual, for the "dance" to begin, but this morning, for the first time, she varied her habit. Always before she had stood reading at the back of the crowd which faced the elevator, waiting for the small woman's touch before she moved forward when the doors slid open.

This morning she did not take her usual place. She stood to one side against the wall and faced outward.

Toward me.

My heart skipped in my chest like a mink on a snowy pond.

She opened her book. I held my breath. The pages of the magazine in my hand fluttered.

Her yellow hair fell straight forward, a blunt line pointing downward from both sides of her chin toward the open book she held one-handed before her. The book cover was dark and my eyes were drawn to the sight of her long middle finger supporting the book's spine. The nail was red, the flesh creamy. She held it straight and firm. My clitoris responded to the sight of that lone finger with a leap that weakened my already trembling knees.

She raised her gaze from her book and engaged my eyes with a look of unmistakable invitation. Her lips curled upward into a killing smile that struck my body like a moving force.

My left hand went of its own volition to rest at my throat, so strong was my physical reaction to the woman's continuing scrutiny. I lost my grip on the magazine and it fell to the floor beside my feet.

She smiled again, this time with brows barely raised, and with a tilting movement of her head made me understand that I was being invited to join her in front of the elevators.

I made my hand leave my throat and rest at my side. With some effort I turned away from her smile, retrieved the magazine and replaced it in the rack. I slowly turned back to see if I had, in my tumbled imaginings, only wished for the notice I had received. Had I made too much of what was merely a friendly acknowledgement? I stood with my gaze cast downward, overcome with doubt. I became acutely aware of the dampened condition of my underwear. I closed my eyes and was transfixed by the overpowering image of that long, red-tipped finger sliding into the buttery wetness between my legs. I trembled and opened my eyes.

She was still there, leaning against the wall beside the elevators, reading.

Or pretending to.

Not yet able to look at her face, I fixed my eyes

upon the book in her hand. The finger along its
spine moved, beckoning me. Twice ... a definite
come-here motion.

I gathered my courage and raised my chin,
looking her full in the eyes. She lowered her lashes,
as if in stunned response to the energy coursing
between us. She held her eyes closed for a moment.
I watched, unable to look away, trapped by my own
boldness. A tiny smile began at one corner of her
red mouth. Then the other side lifted and her lips
parted into a liquid curve. Her tongue moved inside
her mouth, pushing her lips out, slipping quickly
into view, then back again to hide behind strong
white teeth.

She opened her eyes.

I felt the searing effect in the backs of both
knees and in the hollow cave of my stomach.

She motioned again by nodding her head toward
the crowd in front of the elevators.

With great difficulty, I looked away, searching for
the other woman. Where was she? Why was she not
here? My physical condition was worsening by the
moment. Soon I would reach a point of no turning
back. I could feel my whole being straining toward
the freedom from denial, which must — my heart
solidly communicated to my brain — *must* be had,
must be pursued and won for the liberation of my
imprisoned spirit.

I looked back toward her and inclined my head.
She leaned away from the wall and walked to take
her place among the crowd of morning workers. Soon
I stood behind her, the smell of citrus all around me
as I leaned toward her, boldly sucking in the scent

of her shining hair. She turned her head and I knew
it was to ascertain whether or not I was behind her.
Thrills of unimagined proportions gathered in my
lower spine and surged outward, finding exit in my
steaming vagina.

The crowd gathered around us.

I was jostled from behind as the elevator doors
opened, pushed full against her. My body molded to
hers as she leaned back, pressing against my
breasts. I felt them weigh against her back, like two
heated loaves between us. My nipples hardened. I bit
my lip to hold back a sound that gathered like
distant thunder somewhere in the outer regions of
my soul.

The crowd moved into the confines of the bright
cubicle like a square machine made of moving
human parts, all turning about-face at the same
moment. The heat in front of me became a fire
behind me as we turned and I felt *her* breasts press
against *my* back. She fit her knees to the back of
mine and my heart raced. I was in a state of such
extreme excitement that I felt suspended, a
supernova of fiery feeling in a galaxy of burning
suns.

Her hand lay gentle on my hip, unseen in this
box of strangers who were so close I could feel their
body heat. Her fingers pressed lightly, moved around
my waist, then flexed stronger as she pulled my
body tight against hers.

I could barely get my breath but my attention
was wrested away from the waves of pleasure
pulsing between my legs as I experienced a
surprising feeling of closeness from a small woman

who stood in front of me. She pushed back, her buttocks pressing against my groin, rubbing across my pubic mound.

I realized, as I felt her hand reach back, not for mine, but for the hand of the tall one behind me, that I was a prisoner to the rhythmic movements of the two women of my obsession. The muscles of my vagina began to squeeze in time with their movements. My clitoris responded with a thudding, twitching release of such magnitude that I would have fallen into a swoon had I not been held upright between them.

I slumped, in thrall to the absolute pleasure of orgasm, still held firmly by their soft warm bodies.

The tall one whispered against my neck. "Where do you get off?"

The short one turned and smiled, answering for me. "She's not getting off today. We're taking her all the way to the top."

I could only nod, silent with pleasure, hot with the need to taste whatever fruits this new freedom offered. After a lifetime of dwelling in the lower prisons of my dark existence, I was ready for the light. I was . . . going up.

Going with the Weather

Shirley Verel

I had only half noticed her as she had brought her drink out of the crowded bar and gone with it to sit on the grass in the sun, under a sign which said "The Rose and Crown." The hot Saturday lunch time outside the pub had already begun to be dominated for me by the group at the next table, an extended family group, or so it seemed, one of whom was loudly telling the others why it had to be a divorce. "Awkward and foul-tempered and still thinks he's God's gift to women." "But he isn't impotent, then?"

"Don't ask *me*. You could try his personal assistant. Or —"

Well, that was their worry. Anyhow, I had eaten all I wanted of the Dublin Bay prawns in their rustic basket, and the wine was finished, except for the half an inch I had left at the bottom of the bottle as a gesture in the direction of something or other. My idea now was to walk the mile or so across the fields, and go to bed.

I made my way cautiously between the tables to behind the pub, conscious of the effect of the wine, feeling rather white. A stable door was wide open, throwing an ebony shadow onto the rough path. The stable at first had the appearance of being empty. But then I heard a faint sound and, looking, saw a cat in its basket with four kittens. The cat was black.

The kittens couldn't have been born long. The cat was decisive with them, in charge, unsentimental, putting the final touches to their cleanup; it stood no nonsense. Once, it glanced indifferently at me. The kittens mewed, splayed out on their feeble, silky legs, clawed vaguely in the air, crawled over one another.

Yet so soon, I thought, they would be out and about, bucking, frisking, play-acting, laws unto themselves.

I was thinking this when "Thank God for cats," she said. "The country *can* be a bit depressing. For a woman, I mean."

"Can it?" I turned to find her there.

"Well, all those sodding lords of creation. Bulls

and what not down to the sodding roosters — taking
their pick, having their way. You know what I
mean. All those *masters*. Nobody lords it over cats.
Not really. It's why I have one."

She stood for a moment looking at the cat and
its kittens. She didn't say "Aren't they sweet!" or
anything like that, and I was glad.

What she did say at length, turning to me again,
was, "I wondered if you were okay. I thought you
looked a bit —"

"I'm okay."

She hesitated. "So that's all right."

"I'm just going back to the hotel."

"In the village? Are you on holiday?"

"Just the weekend. Are you?" I added, out of
some sort of politeness.

"No, I'm at the University. But I'm living in the
village."

We began to walk together, without any spoken
agreement, towards the stile which led from the pub
to the open fields. There we paused.

"You can see the church," she said. "Someone told
me parts of it are Anglo-Saxon. My name's Caroline,
by the way."

"I'm Val Abbott. And twenty-eight years ago I
was christened in the church you're talking about,
and a quarter of that time I've been in advertising,
and —" I had heard myself with surprise "— will
you, please, make allowances for me because I have
just had a bottle of Chablis in less than an hour
and I'm not used to so much?"

"Nineteen-sixty," she stated. "Why?"

"Nineteen-sixty? Not my decision. Why make allowances? Because women should. For one another."

She nodded. "Why so much today? Wine, I meant."

I looked at her, thinking. Her expression was direct, open, unembarrassed. She had brown hair that turned slightly at her shoulders. She wore makeup, but lightly. Her blue sweater, loose, very thin, gave an impression of breasts, small breasts, rather than displayed them. Why so much wine today? I thought. Well, because perhaps there can come a moment out of the blue when not having a love of one's own anymore feels no longer bearable. But that was a story, unremarkable, over-familiar, hardly to be laid on some chance stranger: the story of an ill-judged passion followed by in the end just one incompatibility too many. So I said instead, "It seemed to go with the weather."

"I know what you mean."

There was a silence.

"But I shan't kill myself on the stile."

"No."

Having climbed the stile, we began our walk across the fields that led to the village, incipient corn, baking in the sun, on either side, and beyond the corn, dilapidated brick walls, and beyond the walls gardens where blossom hung solidly, white, pink, a red deepening almost to claret.

"You smell a little of wine," she said.

"I would, I suppose. I'm sorry."

"It's quite nice. Chablis is."

"You like wine?"

"Yes. Especially when it's hot. Not the wine, the weather."

We must have walked about half a mile, talking here and there, when some unevenness in the ground made me trip, briefly lose my balance, and our hips brushed, and for an instant she put her arm round me, to steady me, and that was what started it. I was aware of catching my breath.

Started what? Oh, I don't know — a sudden longing, I suppose, for all the old, ordinary, incomparable things of the past; a desire, anyway, suddenly so intense that it astonished and possessed me, to put my hand on the tight jeans, feel her movements as she walked, touch her hair, which would be hot from the sun.

She was saying, "I've just read *A Room of One's Own*. For the first time. First times are nice. I must be the last person in my year."

"Virginia Woolf used to live somewhere near here." I had to make myself say something.

"I know she did." She glanced at me.

"Yes — of course."

There was a small wood to go through before reaching the village. It was no cooler, but air came between the trees, warm, like something tangible. Small insects circled in the air.

The instant pick-up, I thought, is relatively easy in advertising copy. Or out of it, no doubt, if you happen to have the knack. Not to mention the courage. And are not too totally out of practice. Is "pick-up" really the word I want? For my situation now?

Then quite soon it seemed that, anyhow, it

wasn't going to matter either way. We had arrived
at the village, at the big, old-fashioned house where
she stopped, saying she lived there — and I had
done nothing.

Only then she said, "Come and see my cat."

A second chance?

The doors inside the house were open, because of
the heat. Her room was an attic, its ceiling acutely
slanted, the window opening almost into a tree just
outside; olive foliage kept light from the room, which
seemed to have the still timelessness of shaded
rooms on hot, sunny days.

The cat was Siamese. It trod fastidiously towards
us, mushroom colored, with darker legs and ears. Its
eyes were the color of her sweater.

"Val — Lucie," she said.

The cat jumped onto the bottom of the divan bed,
curved its claws from the soft paws as if in passing,
made the merest of growls; accepted my caress.

"Do you want some coffee?"

"Please."

"Black?"

I nodded. "Though I'm quite sober now. I like
your mugs." The mugs were a glazed red pottery.
"By the way, I think Lucie is beautiful."

"Yes, well — I'm afraid Lucie is about all I have
to show you."

"Should I go, after the coffee?"

"I have a book somewhere about Virginia. With
pictures."

"I've seen it."

She laughed, then. And, as she waited, her look
gave me courage; the note had been struck.

I said, "I'd be doing this better if we were advertising something."

"Advertising? — Oh, yes, of course. What would you be doing?"

"I don't know. I'd have to think about it. Maybe as an initial idea —" And I put down my mug, and took hers from her, and bracketed her breasts with my hands over her sweater.

She didn't move away. "Because this goes with the weather, too?"

"Something of the sort."

"I suppose I could have been hoping it might." She paused. "Did you guess?"

"I wasn't at all sure."

"What are we advertising?"

"You choose."

"Buttons," she said. And she unbuttoned my shirt, and kissed between my breasts. "You can wait forever for inspiration. So they say."

"Then don't let's wait. Don't let's wait at all. I would so like to make love. What about Lucie?"

"Lucie would so like sardines," she said. It was true — and we claimed the bed for us, and without fuss she wriggled out of her jeans.

"Weren't you hot?"

"Not at crack of dawn."

There was just room for us to lie together on the bed. Her legs were brown, downy; I touched the thighs. Then buried my face, half laughing, in her neck. "Christ, I'm going to be there before anything's happened."

"That's okay." The cat stirred on my skirt. "Has it been a long time? You're not with anyone?"

"Was."

"I've been free-lancing, but —" She stopped. "Hang on so that I can feel it when you come. Could you? I like that."

"I'll try."

Just the feel of her in me was enough.

"Your clitoris is hard." She watched my face, amused, pleased, it seemed. "Now I'm going to do some catching up."

She put my hand where the cross panel of her panties, damp, narrowed, diminished from dampness and heat, cut through the hair; the now faintly, marvelously, sexily odorous hair. My fingers, part imprisoned, the action infinitely pleasurable to me, stroked her beneath it.

She drew in a breath. It was some moments before she said, "We don't need them," and the panties were thrown onto the floor.

Move by move, after that, holding each other, murmuring our pleasure, changing, exchanging positions, we found a converging passion that took us over, went its own way: hand on buttock, lips round nipple, mouth between legs . . .

"Caroline," I said, for the first time.

When at last we got up from the bed it was dusk. Going to the window, I saw, curtailed for me by the tree's foliage, people watering dry flower beds, clipping hedges, one or two on chairs before their front doors, chatting; even listening to the news.

"I'm thirsty. Aren't you?"

"Desperate."

"Orange," she said.

We drank our orange looking out over the village gardens — then heard all at once the clear announcer's voice, which said, "And now for the weather forecast." We looked at each other. "Tomorrow all areas will again be hot." We smiled.

"Good," she said.

The cat stretched, sniffed the air quizzically, closed its gentian eyes.

The Darkroom

Amanda Kyle Williams

Under the dim glow of an infrared light, the
gloved hands rocked the tray gently until only a
faint, buff-colored image remained under
photographic bleach. The print was washed and
submerged in toner. The eyes began to darken, the
mouth redden, the neck — that long, thin, curved
neck — revealed itself in the solution, and the
gloved hands slowly, carefully removed the print
from the tray.

She watched as the print dried, her eyes fixed on

Lisa's image, her concentration so complete that the knock at the door caused her to start.

"Come in." Niki answered her roommate's knock distractedly.

Virginia had taken one step into the darkroom when she saw the photographs drying on the wire. She smiled knowingly. "Obsessing on another one? Jesus, the last one called you daddy when you were lying on top of her. Remember how bad that freaked you out?"

It was true, Niki knew, that she obsessed over her models, that she spent hours studying their photographs, that she turned their flaws to absolute perfection in her lab and then fell in love with them, briefly perhaps, and most of the time only in the privacy of her darkroom, but in love nonetheless.

Virginia patted Niki's head like a puppy. "Let's go out. I need someone to dance with."

Niki shook her head. "I've got a full session with her in the morning for *Secrets*. You know, lace teddies, nightgowns, stuff like that. Thought I should prepare a little. Pretty, huh? Name's Lisa."

Virginia shrugged. "Yeah, well, they've all been pretty. This one straight too? Not that it seems to matter. What is it with you and these women anyway?"

"It's not me," Niki said, suddenly strangely serious, staring at the photographs. "It's something else, something I can't grasp. They love you when you make them beautiful, I think."

Virginia shivered. "That's just too strange, Niki." Turning to leave, she added, "You know, you don't have to lose yourself in them to be a great photographer."

* * * * *

But then there was Lisa ...

She was five-feet-nine inches, short fair hair, large dark eyes. "Nice place." Her voice was silk. "Live alone?"

"No," Niki answered, watching Lisa's back as she dropped her bag on the sofa and walked to the far end of the living room where Niki had set up the lights and props for the session.

"You can change in my room," Niki said. "Last door on —"

"That's okay." The reply came as Lisa was pulling her sweatshirt over her head. Her breasts were small and pretty and very white. Niki smiled, feeling the slight tingle in her stomach and a distinct moistening between her thighs.

Lisa unzipped her jeans and slid them over her hips slowly. "I'd like some music, please, and make it loud."

From the stereo, Melissa Etheridge's husky voice roared "Skin Deep." Niki's autowinder whined. The lights were bright, and Lisa performed exquisitely for the camera. Her dark eyes followed it, caressed it, wanted it. Then a smile, a little pout. She was extraordinary.

"Let the robe fall off one shoulder a little," Niki instructed. "Yeah, that's great. Now let it drag the floor behind you. Head back to show off that gorgeous neck. Perfect." She moved in closer, Lisa's agile body framed in the viewer. "Okay, let's get you on the bed. How about on your side and up on your elbow. Beautiful. Now, look at me and wet your lips a little."

Lisa's tongue made an appearance, circled her lips sensuously and disappeared again. Niki felt her throat tighten. Slowly, she lowered the camera. The tongue made another brief appearance, but this time, Niki knew, it was not for the benefit of the camera.

It had happened like this before. As to why, Niki was not quite certain. What excited them? The music? The lights? The constant hum of the camera? Their own beauty? That their beauty excited her?

She raised the camera and pressed the shutter as Lisa began to move without instruction, pulling the teddy away from one breast, running a licked finger around her nipple until it glistened in the bright lights.

Niki moved closer, the autowinder singing, focusing on the nipple. It was pink and hard and looked like a gumdrop. Niki wanted to touch it, wanted to kiss it, but she was afraid lowering the camera too soon would break the spell.

Lisa was moving again. The teddy was coming off. Her hands moved over her stomach and down into a sparse patch of blond hair.

Niki let out a low groan and gave an encouraging smile from behind the camera. Lisa raised one knee, spreading herself wide. The shutter opened and closed several times, then slowly Niki lowered the camera to the floor and stood.

"Tell me what you want, Lisa," she said quietly, her eyes devouring Lisa's body. "Tell me what you want me to do."

"Touch me," was the soft reply. "I want you to touch me."

Niki closed her eyes for a moment, then moved

to the bed slowly, her eyes never leaving Lisa's. She bent on her knees and ran her hand over Lisa's smooth stomach. Lisa's warm hand took Niki's chin, guiding her mouth, kissing her deeply. Niki pressed herself hard against the bed, feeling the denim seam rubbing against her. She let the kiss go on until Lisa's breath turned to staggered gasps, until she could feel Lisa's desire completely, and then she pulled away, standing, carefully opening her belt buckle and pulling the thin brown belt from its loops. Lisa reached for Niki's thigh. Niki took her wrist gently but firmly.

"Give me the other one," she directed, and Lisa complied without hesitation, holding up both wrists. Niki smiled and pulled the wrists over Lisa's head, then tightened the belt expertly around the headboard.

Lisa's eyes were half closed when Niki returned to her. She ran her tongue over Lisa's neck, around the curve of the ear, and whispered, "I'm going to make love to you, Lisa. Is that what you want?"

"Yes," Lisa whispered back, her body arching, her hips grinding into the bed.

Niki moved her hand between Lisa's legs, coating a finger with the warm, milky evidence of Lisa's excitement, then brought it to Lisa's breasts, making small circles around the nipples. She could smell Lisa's passion. The scent filled her nostrils with sweet, musky memories, memories of love, memories of sex, memories of others who had given themselves willingly and deliberately on this bed, in her bedroom, her darkroom, her kitchen. She ached to dive into Lisa, but tried to impose some discipline on herself. Go slow, she told herself, go slow and it will last longer. But the thoughts were fleeting and there was, after all, Lisa's heavy breath on her neck, Lisa's silky voice pleading for more, Lisa's eyes watching her expectantly. And when, at last, she pressed her head between Lisa's legs, when she ran her tongue over the blond hair and around the soft, pink flesh, when she inserted a finger and felt the muscles tighten, she heard Lisa moan, heard Lisa say her name softly again and again, and for just a moment she thought she heard Lisa say, "You're mine."

Lisa left the apartment around two that afternoon and Niki left shortly after. It was well after dark when Niki returned to find Virginia sitting on the couch watching television and the apartment smelling of baked chicken and garlic.

"What's cooking?" Niki asked, plopping herself on the couch.

"You tell me. I thought we made an agreement to discuss it before we handed out keys to the place." Virginia was obviously annoyed. "I came home and *Lisa* was in the kitchen cooking. She questioned me about our relationship, gave me a glass of wine and told me dinner would be in an hour."

"I didn't give her a key," Niki whispered.

"Well, she's got one, girl. She told me she let herself in."

Niki stared at her for a moment. "She took my car and got us some lunch earlier. She must have made a copy. But why?"

"So I could surprise you with dinner," Lisa said, emerging from the kitchen. "Have a good afternoon? I did, thanks to you." She kissed Niki passionately, then produced the key. "Here you go."

She vanished into the kitchen and Niki looked at Virginia nervously. "See it's no big deal. Just a surprise."

Virginia smiled and punched Niki's arm playfully. "Does she call you daddy?"

Whatever there was of Lisa's life before she came to Niki's bed was a bit of a mystery. She offered little about her past. She apparently had no commitments, she made no phone calls to lovers or roommates or family who might be concerned for her whereabouts. And this bit of mystery seemed to add excitement to the first days of their affair. Lisa seemed fascinated with Niki's photography, she loved to watch Niki work in her darkroom, loved it when they were naked and Niki spread her legs and asked for Lisa's fingers in the dim red light, loved it when they moved to Niki's private little corner of the living room where the lights were blinding, where the bed was soft and the belt was strong. And in the night, Lisa's warm body pressed against Niki, her tongue slipped between Niki's thighs expertly in the mornings, her voice whispered suggestions into Niki's ears in the afternoons that kept her in a constant state of arousal. But on the fourth day, Niki suddenly began to tire of the arrangement, as she often did after the initial infatuation.

"Lisa, these last few days have been wonderful,

really, but it's time for me to get back to work. I've got a shoot this morning at eleven. Why don't I call you later?"

Lisa smiled and touched Niki's cheek lightly. "I'll be as quiet as a mouse. You won't even know I'm here."

"But I *will* know you're here. Listen," Niki sighed and tried to make her voice soft. "I need some time, time for work, time to myself. Don't you need that too?"

Lisa's big eyes searched Niki's face innocently. "Don't you love me?"

"You're a beautiful woman, Lisa, but I need some time. Okay? Just a little time?"

Lisa's dark eyes hardened at that. "There's someone else, isn't there, some bitch you're fucking at eleven."

Niki looked at her in utter horror. No words would come. She sat there stunned. Suddenly Lisa seemed to recover. She smiled softly. "Of course, darling. I understand. Just call me later."

Niki nodded and watched her leave, then went to the fridge for some juice. On the top shelf, she found a note.

I love you, Lisa

Later, after returning from an afternoon meeting, Niki turned her key in the latch and opened the door. Then a sound from the rear of the apartment ... Breathing, heavy, erratic, then a woman's quiet, childlike sobbing.

"My God," she whispered, and started slowly down the hallway.

At her bedroom door, she stopped, staring in disbelief at the destruction. The pillows and sheets had been shredded. The framed photographs on her wall had been knocked down, the glass broken and some of her best work slit and torn apart mercilessly.

Then a crash from the walk-in closet she had converted to a darkroom. She closed her eyes. *Oh God, she's tearinq my darkroom apart. Think. Okay, this woman is obviously disturbed. She probably has a knife, broken glass, something awful. Shit ... Call 911. That's it. Call the fucking police.*

She hurried quietly down the hallway, her heart pounding against her chest. She reached for the phone, hands trembling, and tried to find her voice. "This is Nicole Michalosky," she whispered. "Someone's in my apartment. I'm at twelve fifty-four Thirteenth Street. Please hurry. She's tearing the place to —"

A shadow ... A quiet footstep ... She spun around and saw Lisa standing behind her, a kitchen knife in her hand. There was blood on her arms. She was smiling. *Oh God, she's smiling.*

Niki held both hands in front of her and took a step back. "Okay, now listen to me, Lisa. I want to help you. Just stay calm. Everything's going to be fine."

The hand with the knife moved slightly. "No, Niki, everything *was* fine. But you ruined it. Don't you see?" Lisa spoke softly, patiently, as if she were explaining something to a very small child.

Don't look afraid. Stay calm. Keep her talking until the police come.

"I missed you, Lisa," she said suddenly, wondering where the words had come from. "I missed you a lot. I was going to call later, ask you to come over. I wanted you tonight."

It seemed to be working. The hand with the knife was back at Lisa's side, her eyes were fixed on Niki. *Keep talking.*

"Do you know what I was thinking? I was thinking we could go out, you know, actually out for dinner. We could make love in the car on the way home. I know a spot —"

The door opened. It all happened so fast Niki could scarcely sort it out. Lisa raised the knife and ran shrieking towards Virginia who froze at the sight of her. Niki grabbed Lisa's arm. They were all screaming by now, Virginia in shock, Niki in utter terror, Lisa in complete rage.

By the time the police arrived Niki was standing against the wall with the knife in her hand watching Lisa. Lisa was in a fetal position on the couch crying, long trails of black mascara streaked her face. Virginia was sitting on the coffee table with a cloth over a nasty cut on her forearm and a mixture of disgust and total fury on her face.

It took quite a long time for Niki to repair the damage done by her possessive lover, the damage done to her friendship with Virginia, who had, understandably, decided to move out. The damage done to her financially — the darkroom, the lights, the cameras — and, of course, the psychological damage. It would be extremely difficult to trust a lover again, difficult to take a lover so casually.

Under the dim glow of an infrared light, the gloved hands rocked the tray gently until only a slight buff-colored image remained in photographic bleach. The print was washed and submerged in toner. The eyes began to darken, the mouth redden.

Niki smiled.

Then there was Helen ...

Triple A

Molleen Zanger

We call each other friend. As in "I'm having lunch with a friend" or "I was talking to a friend of mine" or "A friend of mine and I are going shopping."

We go shopping. A stupid thing to do with a woman like Sylvia. I feel like the eighth dwarf next to Sylvia.

Frumpy. Short and squat and frumpy. And poor and stupid and inept.

I never trip unless I am with Sylvia. With her, I

dribble soup as if I held a trick spoon. With her I belch, or hiccup. With her I trail a yard of toilet paper stuck to my shoe from the ladies' room floor.

Her house is bigger, her dog is cuter, her woman more fun at parties. She went to college longer, never smoked and never busts the zippers of her jeans.

None of which gives her pride; the only thing she is really proud of are her damned narrow feet.

Her feet are so narrow, she laments smugly, that she has to drive all the way to Lansing to find a pair to fit. There is one store, Ayla's Shoes, that stocks her size. But they are so expensive, she complains proudly, she can only buy them on sale, four or five pairs at a time.

They send her a pink postcard informing her, a preferred customer, of the big end-of-season sale. Half off and more!

And so I go with her to Lansing. I drive my pathetic little '84 Renault because her BMW is in the shop again.

I want badly to hate Sylvia, my friend. I can't. She's marvelous. She's everything I can't be. And she likes me! She thinks I am funny and "original." I make her laugh. For this she rewards me with friendship. She calls me friend. Sometimes she strokes my hand, or fixes my collar, tucking in a tag. Sometimes she stands very close to me as she talks to me and I am sure, so sure she is going to kiss me. Then she laughs and straightens, pulling away, and I think I imagined it. Of course I did. Why would she want me with my sagging breasts and the protuberant belly sit-ups will not fix? But I want her and an instinct tells me I do not imagine things. So I go with her anywhere she invites me.

Even shopping. Even shopping for shoes.

We barely get on the expressway and I feel the tension in the car. She is flushed and talking excitedly. She gestures with her hands, touching my arm often. Even touching my thigh. For emphasis, of course. She is nervous, aroused. She loves buying narrow shoes for her narrow feet.

There is a parking place right in front of the store. I think it is reserved for her. I think the store manager runs out of the store and shoos away people who would park there.

I hear him say, "Go away! You can't park here! Sylvia's coming!"

I hear them say, "Oh, gee, today? Gosh, I'm sorry, hey — I'll just park down in the next block. Sorry fella."

As we step into the store, Sylvia stops still, closes her eyes and tries to breathe slowly. She doesn't want to peak too soon.

The manager himself greets her, ushers her to a chair. Not Us. Her. I am invisible. It happened at the threshold. He cannot see me. He knows I do not buy. He knows, I think, the balance in my checkbook, the negative numbers lurking there. He knows how long it has been since I mopped my kitchen floor and he knows that I do not spend in a year what Sylvia will spend on one pair of his shoes, even at half off and more.

I sit beside her, it is my duty to tell her how beautiful the shoes are, how beautiful they look on her feet. She clasps my hand as the manager turns his back, goes to get another pair. Her hand is cold, clammy. It trembles slightly. Then he comes back balancing boxes like coffins for dolls.

She tries on every pair he brings her. Every color, every style. The prices astound me. I cannot speak. I nod yes, I like them.

Black patent pumps with impossibly high thin heels, rhinestones embedded all around the edge. Garish in the box; elegant on Sylvia.

Brown suede "walking" shoes, still two and a half inches in the heel. Crushed brown suede, like velvet.

And red, bright red, lizard heels with sharp toes. I have never seen shoes as beautiful. I gasp as she slips them on her narrow feet. She looks at me strangely and smiles, her eyes narrowing. She looks at me, directly, frankly, and says to him, "I'll take these" and then she covers my hand with hers, right in front of him. And then she tells him she will also take the black ones and the butter yellow, butter-soft flats and the gray ones with the stacked heels.

She hands him her credit card; he hands me the bags, each shoebox in its own drawstringed bag. He opens the door for her and I stumble over the metal strip at the threshold, falling after her.

In the car, as I am backing out, she asks if I want anything. She looks at me and I know she knows what I want, exactly what I want. And I feel in a piercing needle of truth that she wants that too.

She says, shall we get some coffee or something here or shall we go to my house? She says it so offhandedly. I take my cue from her.

"Oh, let's go to your house," I say. "We can kick off our shoes," I say.

She is looking straight ahead but I see her smile.
I see my half of her smile.

All the way home she smiles. She is quiet now,
smiling.

At her house I fumble for her packages, an
eager, willing lackey.

Her woman opens the door. She is smiling, too.

"Have a good time, you two?" she smiles.

"Yes, but we're exhausted," Sylvia smiles, "Let's
all have some coffee, put our feet up."

I shove the bags into her woman's hands,
mumble something, I don't know what, I have to go
home, something like that.

I am not quite crying, but close, as I put my car
in the garage. As I climb out, tangling my jacket
fringe in the emergency brake, I see in the back
seat a drawstring bag. The bag says Ayla's Shoes. It
says Sylvia's Shoes.

I take the package into the house and straight
up to my room. Still choking back tears, I tear open
the bag — really tearing the bag open — not
opening it at the top. I pour the simmering shoes
onto the bed. They look like they are still living
things. Lizards, impossible red lizards.

I dial Sylvia's number and it rings seven eight
nine ten times before someone clatters it off its
hook. Two voices laugh and laugh but no one says
hello. I hang up and dial back. The phone is busy.
Sylvia is busy.

I stroke the narrow, narrow shoes. I try to fit
them on my feet. It is absurd how narrow these
shoes look, but they are still beautiful without Sylvia
in them.

I take off my clothes, frumpy clothes. I fit one

hand into each shoe, too narrow even for my hand, but I squeeze.

I stroke my bare flesh with expensive lizard shoes. My shoulders, my neck, down across my breasts, pinching nipples with sharp heels. I think of Sylvia's feet and Sylvia's hands and Sylvia's smile as I rub the shoes against my skin. Down and down, now one in front, one in back, across my ass and between my legs. I drop the one in back, use both hands now in front. I rub and rub harder and harder and deeper. I feel every scale of the lizard shoes. I feel the cold metal stud at the toe, on the sole. I feel Sylvia's hand on me and it is she who slowly slides the narrow narrow shoe the beautiful red shoe slowly slowly into me deeper and deeper I feel the narrow heel sharp against my ass and the shoe the whole shoe is there to the heel and it is Sylvia who watches me come.

The Road To Healing Heart

Jeane Harris

Looking back on it, Ellen Kramer decided that the day she let her friends Storm and Dana talk her into getting a massage was one of the most depressing days of her life. Not that any of the previous days in recent memory had much to recommend them.

She was sitting in Storm's backyard watching her trim her lawn with a pair of hedge clippers while

Dana splashed around naked with her two Dobermans in a small plastic wading pool. It was a strange scene that seemed entirely in keeping with the unreal heat and humidity that had descended on central Missouri earlier in the week.

Ellen watched her two friends from the back steps where she sat drinking a lukewarm beer. Her tank top was drenched with sweat, she had an agonizing case of cramps, a miserable summer cold, and she was brooding about the previous evening at the bar when she had seen her ex-lover, Karen, dancing with her latest love interest, Gabriella. Karen had broken up with Ellen four months before and the pain of their separation after six years together was a raw wound that still ached every time she saw Karen with someone else. She knew that Storm and Dana were worried about her which was why they had invited her over, why they called her every day and no doubt would soon start trying to fix her up with some friend of theirs.

Ellen leaned against the screen door and drained the last of her beer. She blew her nose into her damp bandanna and exhaled. "Jesus Christ, it's so fucking hot."

"Come get in with us," Dana called to her. Dana was sprawled out in the pool, a Doberman on either side of her.

"I can't," Ellen said. "My menstrual cramps have paralyzed me from the waist down." She sneezed explosively and again wiped her sore, chapped nose.

Storm looked up from her lawn trimming and pushed a tendril of damp hair from her eyes. "I can make you some chamomile tea. It's very good for cramps and it's a good decongestant too."

Ellen eyed Storm warily. "No thanks. I need something stronger than tea. Like morphine."

"I have some Dristan upstairs," Dana offered.

"I don't want anything." Ellen shook her empty beer can. "Well, maybe another beer."

"You just want to bitch," Dana said.

"Well, I have every right to bitch, don't I?" she said harshly. "The woman I love left me, I have life-threatening menstrual cramps, a miserable cold . . . and no beer." She rose and went into the kitchen.

Dana and Storm exchanged a meaningful look.

"Well?" Dana asked.

Storm shrugged and moved to another section of lawn. "Perhaps. Let's talk to her some more."

"Talk to me about what?" Ellen asked, emerging from the house with a beer in her hand.

Dana stood up and began toweling herself off. "Aren't you worried that the neighbors will see you?" Ellen asked her.

Dana laughed and wrapped the towel around her waist. "Who? Ginny? Vanessa? Cassandra? Everybody who lives on this block is a dyke. They've seen me naked before." She sat down beside Ellen and put her arm around her friend.

"You're still hurting, aren't you, babe?"

Ellen nodded and to her alarm felt tears rolling down her cheeks. She wiped at them roughly with the back of her hand.

"It's okay," Dana said, pulling Ellen's head down to her shoulder. "Crying is good. Crying is okay."

"I'm *not* crying," Ellen said, shaking her head. "It's just this damn cold."

Storm put down the hedge clippers. "Maybe a massage would make you feel better."

Ellen looked at her doubtfully. "A massage?"

"Yes," Storm said, arranging her skirt around her ankles demurely. "A massage can be a very ... healing experience. If nothing else, it will relax you and release a lot of the tension and hurt you're feeling right now."

"And where am I supposed to get this massage?" Ellen asked sarcastically. "Kitty's Pleasure Palace next to the tattoo parlor?"

Dana shoved her playfully. "Of course not, you bozo. We know someone who gives massages." She looked at Storm. "I have her card around here somewhere."

"I dunno," Ellen said doubtfully. "I don't think I'm a massage-type of person."

Storm smiled at Ellen indulgently. "And what exactly is a massage type person?"

Dana nudged Ellen. "This is a trick question."

"I know," Ellen mumbled. "She's got that teacher tone in her voice. I don't know, Storm. Hippie-trippy granola lesbians like you and Dana?"

Dana laughed. "Hey, I like that. Granola lesbians." She laughed again and went into the house.

Storm smoothed her skirt over her knees. "Truly Ellen, you will enjoy the massage. Indigo is a very remarkable woman."

"Indigo?" Ellen repeated. "Her name is Indigo?"

"Yeah," Dana said, emerging from the house with a small gray card in her hand. "Cool name, huh?"

Ellen took the card. Simple block letters spelled out one word: INDIGO. Below the single name, *Creative bodywork and massage.* And in the lower right-hand corner an address: *25 Healing Heart Road.*

Ellen snickered. "Healing Heart Road. Where's that? Down at the end of Lonely Street?"

"It's off Baseline," Dana said. "It's kind of hard to find."

"If I decide to do this, I'll just call Indigo and get directions from her." Ellen turned the card over. "Hey, there's no phone number on here."

"She doesn't have a phone," Storm said softly.

"Then how the hell am I supposed to make an appointment?"

"You don't need an appointment," Dana told her. "Just drive out there. She's always home." Dana looked at Storm for support.

Storm got up and came over to Ellen. Squatting down in front of her, she took Ellen's hands in her own strong, brown hands. "Ellen, we love you and we want you to feel better. I promise you, after seeing Indigo, you will feel *much* better." She smiled what Dana called her Mother Earth smile.

"You aren't pulling my leg about this Healing Heart Road, are you? This isn't like a snipe hunt or anything?"

"We wouldn't kid about something as serious as your heart," Storm said, turning back to her clippers.

It was odd, Ellen decided later, because she was certain that she hadn't made a conscious decision to get a massage from Indigo. However, three days after her evening at Dana and Storm's, she was

looking for something to eat and saw the card stuck
behind a magnet on her refrigerator.

INDIGO.

Without thinking about it, Ellen tucked the card
in her pocket, grabbed her car keys.

She turned off onto a narrow dirt road lined with
thick woods that thinned every so often so the silver
ribbon of river was visible through the trees. When
she was five miles past the general store without
having seen the oak tree Storm had described to
her, Ellen turned around and drove back to the
store, wondering how she had missed something
Storm had described as enormous. Oddly enough, on
her second trip down the dirt road, there it was.
And it *was* enormous — a huge, gnarled monster of
a tree spreading its canopy out halfway across the
road.

"Now how could I have missed this?" Ellen asked
herself.

She parked the car under the tree and got out.
The air was at least ten degrees cooler outside the
car, and Ellen breathed a sigh of relief. She walked
around the tree looking for the sign that Storm had
told her about. On her second circle, she finally saw
it; it was the color of the tree trunk and looked as
old; soft, weathered letters that read: HEALING
HEART ROAD. An arrow pointed off to the left.
Ellen looked, saw no road, blinked, and then there
was a road. Sort of. A green tunnel through dense
underbrush and saplings.

"Oh, this is too weird," Ellen said to herself. "I'll
never be able to drive through there." But when she
got back into her car and approached the tunnel

through the trees, it seemed wider and the branches parted, or so it seemed, to let the car through. To call it a road was a bit of an exaggeration — two ruts nearly overgrown with grass — but it was discernible. After ten minutes the ruts suddenly ended. One minute they were visible and the next the forest was there — an impenetrable wall. Ellen sighed, stopped the car and got out. As she walked toward the trees, she saw a path, faint and overgrown but there.

"I can't believe I'm actually doing this," she muttered, locking her car and pocketing the keys.

But it was wonderfully cool in the woods. As she walked along, she heard the faint tapping of a woodpecker, and the shrilling insect sounds which had been strangely absent when she first got out of the car.

After she had walked for about five minutes, she noticed that the trees were thinning out and a little further on the path emerged from the woods. She saw a small garden, neatly mulched with straw and surrounded by a driftwood fence. Smooth river stones in strange, abstract designs were laid out next to the garden. Even though it was only June, the corn stood tall and green, the ears silked out and fat. A string hammock hung between two trees, beside a wooden bucket half full of water and an assortment of garden tools.

But she saw no cabin as Dana and Storm had promised.

She walked on and then suddenly she did spy a small building, though it was too small to be called a cabin. A hexagonal wooden structure with a mud and stick roof, it reminded Ellen of Navajo hogans that she had seen once on a trip through New Mexico.

"Hello?" Ellen called out, feeling foolish. "Anybody here?"

"Hi," a cheerful voice said from behind her. Ellen whirled around to see a woman standing in the middle of the garden. Ellen was certain she hadn't been there a minute ago.

"Hi," Ellen said, walking toward her. As she neared the woman, she was astounded to see how young and beautiful she was. She didn't know what she had expected — certainly someone older, maybe Storm's age.

Indigo was perhaps twenty-five, with an unruly mane of light brown hair. Her low-cut white peasant blouse was smudged with dirt, and her jeans showed that she had been kneeling in the garden.

"I'm Ellen Kramer, a friend of Dana and Storm. They gave me your card." Ellen fished around in her pocket and found the card, now crumpled and damp. She held it out to Indigo who laughed and waved it away.

"Great," she said. "I'm glad they shared it with you. You keep it."

Up close to Indigo, Ellen was overwhelmed with how lovely she was. Her eyes were a startling, impossible blue, fringed with thick dark eyelashes, her cheekbones were high and arching, her mouth wide and generous. Light brown freckles stood out against the darker brown of her face. When she took Ellen's hand, Ellen felt a warm tingling in her arm.

"Are you here for a massage?" Indigo asked in a friendly tone.

Ellen couldn't stop staring at her. She was enchanted by her beautiful eyes, her full lips; she knew she was staring but couldn't stop herself.

"Uh, yeah. Is that ... okay? I mean, do you have time?"

Indigo laughed, a happy, musical sound like water over river stones. "Time is one thing I have a lot of." She ducked under the fence. "Your name is Ellen?" Indigo slipped her arm around Ellen's waist in a familiar yet entirely natural way and began walking toward the cabin. Ellen was acutely aware of Indigo's breasts swaying freely against her arm as they walked.

At the porch of the cabin, Indigo dropped her arm, and Ellen felt the absence of her touch. She watched as Indigo washed her hands in a basin by the door.

"Did you have any trouble finding the turnoff?" Indigo asked, drying her hands.

"No — well, a little," Ellen said, admiring Indigo's brown, well-muscled arms. "I missed the oak tree the first time down the road, but I found it okay."

Indigo opened the door to the cabin. "Come on in."

Ellen followed her inside the dark cabin; its air was close and warm. The windows were screened in, wooden shutters propped up outside. On one of the six walls stood a small stone fireplace with a stack of kindling on the hearth. The floor was also stone with Indian blankets scattered around. The furniture consisted of only a padded table with two sheets folded across the end.

"That's my massage table." Indigo turned away

and busied herself with some bottles on a shelf beside the table. Ellen stood in the center of the room, uncertain what to do next. She looked around the room, puzzled by its bareness. Where did the woman eat? Where was the stove, refrigerator, plates, dishes? Bathroom?

"I'm going to put on some music, if that's okay with you," Indigo said, inserting a cassette tape into a portable tape player. "It's Coyote Woman. Have you heard her music?"

"I don't think so," Ellen said.

"Her music helps me relax and prepare myself."

"Uh, how many . . . should I take off my clothes?" Ellen asked. The question sounded stupid to her now that she had asked it.

Indigo's teeth flashed in the dim light of the cabin. "As many as you feel comfortable taking off," she said. "You really get the most benefit from a massage if you take them all off." She motioned toward the sheets on the table. "Only the part of your body that I'm working on at the time will be exposed."

Ellen hurriedly stripped off her clothes, wishing now that she had kept off the twenty pounds she'd lost a few years ago.

"Do you mind if I take off some of my clothes?" Indigo asked from behind her. "What I do is really strenuous and it's warm in here."

Ellen felt her face burning. "Uh, yeah, I mean, no, of course not. Yeah, It's really warm." She turned away, feeling stupid. She and her friends often swam naked in a secluded swimming hole out in the country, and she went naked at the music

festival in Michigan each year. But the thought of
seeing this particular woman naked in this tiny, hot
cabin, was unbearable.

As she was taking off the last of her clothes,
Ellen noticed a pungent smell, strong yet pleasant.
She turned around to see Indigo rubbing some oil
into her hands. She had taken off her blue jeans.

"You have a beautiful body," Indigo said easily,
as though she were admiring a sunset. There was
absolutely nothing suggestive or sexual in her voice
but Ellen was still flustered. "Get up on the table
and let's get started."

Ellen walked across the room, climbed onto the
table and lay face down, pulling the sheet over
herself. There was an opening in the table for her
face. A curious peace settled over her. The music
from the cassette player was strange, ethereal. She
heard Indigo humming softly to herself and sensed
movement beside her. The sheet that covered her
was gently removed and, as her eyes strained to see
what Indigo was doing, suddenly, electrically, she felt
a strong, warm hand in the small of her back and
then one on the back of her head. The pressure was
faint at first, then Indigo seemed to rock back and
forth, pressing down first on her back and then on
her head.

"What I'm doing right now is finding the center
of the music with your body." Indigo's low voice
seemed part of the music now, like Coyote Woman's
flute.

Then her hands were no longer on Ellen's back
but on her scalp, working beneath her hair,
massaging the tension that Ellen was not even

aware of until Indigo's hands told her that the tension was leaving her. The nagging headache that had accompanied her cold was gone, gone as quietly and swiftly as the fading notes of Coyote Woman's flute into the still, warm air. The sensation of Indigo's fingers kneading her scalp, neck and shoulders was so exquisite that Ellen felt the wetness growing between her legs.

Indigo's hands moved down her shoulders, to her back, buttocks and legs and finally to her feet, gently, and sometimes not so gently, kneading and stroking, moving to her toes, running her strong, knowing fingers between each toe, tugging on each one and then moving to her feet, massaging away the knots of frustration. She felt Indigo pick up her leg, rest it on her shoulder and run her hands down the length of her leg. Then, lifting the sheet, Indigo began massaging her upper thigh, her fingers grazing the inside of Ellen's leg and trailing into the wetness that Ellen knew must surely be there. The second time Indigo's fingers touched her, Ellen heard herself groan and felt her face flush with excitement and embarrassment.

But Indigo only murmured sympathetically. "It does feel good, doesn't it?"

Suddenly, the exquisite sensations, the incredible pleasure became too much for Ellen and something inside her burst, like a dam, and she began to cry. Huge sobs racked her body. She tried to stop but found it impossible. Embarrassed by her sobs, Ellen nevertheless felt an overwhelming relief. She imagined the pain leaving her body as if a huge, dark bird had lifted off and flown away.

Indigo did not speak or try to comfort her

verbally; instead she came to the head of the table and helped Ellen turn over. Then, gathering her into her arms, she held Ellen to her breast and rocked her like a baby.

"It's all right now," she whispered. "This happens a lot when I do bodywork on people who have been deeply hurt."

Ellen tried to speak, found she couldn't and stopped trying.

"You've been wounded, your body knows that, it needs release from pain as much as your mind," Indigo whispered in her ear.

Ellen dried her face on the sheet. She started to pull back, but Indigo's face was so close and her lips so near. Ellen reached up, caught the back of Indigo's neck and pulled her face down. Indigo's lips were as soft and yielding as Ellen had imagined they would be.

Ellen pulled back. "I'm sorry. I couldn't seem to help myself."

Indigo smiled. She reached up and untied the knot that held the front of her peasant blouse together. Ellen watched as the blouse slid off her smooth, brown shoulders, revealing full breasts with pink nipples. "Sex is very healing too," she said, and guided Ellen's mouth toward her. Indigo's breasts were warm, her nipples hard. And although sucking Indigo's nipples was an incredibly sexual experience, there was also something comforting about it. Ellen didn't feel, as she often did at this point in love-making, the need to hurry and do something else. Ellen knew somehow that her hungry mouth was giving Indigo as much pleasure as it was giving her.

Time seemed elongated. Ellen moved leisurely

back and forth from one breast to the other, her mouth sucking harder and harder, pulling Indigo's nipples deeper and deeper into her mouth. Indigo moaned and whimpered as Ellen sucked harder and she finally fell forward on top of Ellen. Ellen struggled to move the sheet that separated them and then watched appreciatively as Indigo slipped out of her underpants and maneuvered herself under Ellen, so that Ellen was straddling her.

The cabin was stiflingly hot, and sweat glistened on their naked bodies, lubricating them as they slid against each other on the tangled sheets. Ellen opened her eyes and saw Indigo's face below her, flushed with excitement. She felt her own swollen labia and clitoris rubbing against Indigo's sweat-slicked thigh as she moved up and down on her leg. Ellen reached down and parted her own lips; she was so wet that her fingers slipped inside, and she ground her hips against Indigo's leg, forcing her fingers deeper.

Indigo drew Ellen's head down to kiss her again and their mouths crushed together, teeth clicking, tongues thrusting into each other's mouths. Ellen drew away, gasping, and lifted her body off Indigo's leg. Her own fingers slipped out and she frantically thrust Indigo's hand between her legs. Indigo understood and pushed her fingers deep inside Ellen and watched as Ellen braced herself, one hand on either side of Indigo's head. Raising her hips slowly, Ellen let Indigo's fingers slowly slip out of her, and then tantalizingly, inch by agonizing inch, she lowered herself back down again.

Indigo kept up the pressure by holding her leg steady and keeping her hand firm in the small of

Ellen's back. Suddenly, as Ellen lowered herself one last time, she threw her head back and her throat began working wordlessly. Ellen's hips moved frantically up and down, pushing Indigo's fingers deeper and deeper into her. Ellen felt her orgasm gathering, grasping at Indigo's fingers, and heard herself moaning, the moan turning into a cry of orgasmic release. Dimly, at the outer edges of her consciousness, Ellen was aware that the music of Coyote Woman had reached some sort of crescendo, and she collapsed forward, her head on Indigo's bare breasts. Indigo's hands stroked her back gently and she kissed Ellen's forehead soothingly.

"I want to make love to you too," Ellen said. "I want to taste you."

Indigo smiled and her kiss told Ellen everything she wanted to know. As Ellen trailed kisses down Indigo's flat belly, the tape clicked on and the haunting, surreal music of Coyote Woman began again. Ellen smiled and lowered her head.

It was nearly dark when they walked back to the path that led into the forest. Indigo handed Ellen a lantern.

"Don't you believe in flashlights?" Ellen asked teasingly.

Indigo merely smiled. "Just hang it on a tree branch when you reach your car. Someone will bring it back to me."

Ellen kissed her and held her close for a moment. "Thank you. I don't feel ... broken anymore. Healed, I guess."

Indigo hugged her tightly and then moved away toward her garden. "I'm glad," she said. The shadows were long and deep, and as Ellen turned away, she saw Indigo duck under the fence and disappear into the shadows. It was an eerie sight, as though Indigo had been absorbed by the shadows. She shook her head at this fanciful thought.

But she didn't look back.

A week later, Ellen again sat on the back steps of Storm and Dana's house.

"You certainly seem happier," Dana observed from the wading pool.

"I was thinking about going back to Indigo for another massage," Ellen said.

Storm, who was pulling weeds in her flower garden, looked up at Ellen. "You can't go back, sweetie. You can only go to Indigo once."

Ellen thought of the afternoon she had spent in Indigo's cabin and how Indigo had seemed to melt into the shadowy garden. She also remembered the way the forest had closed behind her as she walked back to her car, and that when she had turned around at her car, the path wasn't there anymore.

"Yeah, I see what you mean." She pulled out the small card that Indigo had insisted she keep. "So the deal is, I give this to someone who needs it, too?"

Storm nodded. "That's the idea."

"Hey, Storm?"

"What?"

"Did you and Dana ... I guess you've both been with Indigo."

"I got my card from Ginny. I met Dana right after I went to see Indigo. Dana was still hurting a lot from her mother's death and her breakup with Christina." She turned back to Ellen and smiled. "I gave Dana the card Ginny gave me."

On the Authors

NIKKI BAKER is the author of two mystery novels featuring African-American protagonist Virginia Kelly: *In the Game* and *The Lavender House Murder*. She is completing a third novel in the series, *Long Goodbyes*, to be published by The Naiad Press in 1993. Baker lives in Chicago, Illinois.

JACKIE CALHOUN is the author of *Lifestyles*, *Second Chance*, and *Sticks and Stones*. Her fourth book, *Friends and Lovers*, is scheduled for publication in 1993. She makes her home in Wisconsin's Fox River Valley, while spending as much time as possible at her lake cottage near Wild Rose. She is presently at work on her fifth novel.

RHONDA DICKSION is the author of Naiad Press's *The Lesbian Survival Manual* and the forthcoming *Stay Tooned,* both collections of her popular cartoon panels, which appear in publications nationwide. She and her partner live in a rural area of Washington State and spend their time exploring and appreciating the majestic peaks and lush valleys that abound around them.

LAUREN WRIGHT DOUGLAS was born in 1947, in Canada. She grew up in a military family and spent part of her childhood in Europe. She began telling stories to her cat at an early age and published her first short story in the school newspaper at age twelve. She recalls nothing about it except that it was very long and very bad. Despite professional detours into teaching, journalism, finance, translation, and editing, Lauren has been writing ever since. Her novels for Naiad Press include *The Always Anonymous Beast, Osten's Bay* (as Zenobia Vole), *In the Blood, Ninth Life* (winner of the 1990 Lambda Literary Award for Best Lesbian Mystery), *The Daughters of Artemis,* and *A Tiger's*

Heart. Her new novel *Goblin Market* will be published by Naiad in 1993 as will *To Steal Your Heart Away,* a collection of short stories. Lauren lives in Southern California with her partner and an ever-changing number of cats, to whom she still tells stories.

JENNIFER FULTON is a full-time writer living in the windiest city in the world — Wellington, New Zealand. Her first romance, *Passion Bay,* was published in 1992 and her second, *True Love,* will follow in 1993. As alter ego Rose Beecham, Jennifer smokes cigars, drives too fast, and writes the Amanda Valentine mysteries. Apart from writing, Jennifer's favorite self-indulgences are fly-fishing, travel and gourmet cooking. Between books, she can be quite charming to family, friends, felines and phone-callers.

JEANE HARRIS is an Associate Professor of English at Arkansas State University where she is the Director of Freshman English. She has a twenty-two-year-old son, Scholfield, who is a computer science major and a partner, Lisa, who is in the doctoral program in English and folklore at the University of Missouri. The rear end of her cat, Socrates, remains the size of a Buick, though recent efforts have reduced her bulk somewhat.

The author of *Black Iris* and *Delia Ironfoot,* Jeane Harris's next Naiad release is scheduled for 1994 and will be a second Delia Ironfoot adventure, *Women of the Red Sky.*

PENNY HAYES was born in Johnson City, New York, in February, 1940. As a child she lived on a farm near Binghamton, New York. She later attended school in Utica and Buffalo, graduating with degrees in art and special education. She has made her living teaching in both New York State and West Virginia. She presently resides in Ithaca, New York.

Ms. Hayes' interests include backpacking, mountain climbing, canoeing, traveling, reading, gardening and studying early American history.

She has been published in *I Know You Know, Of the Summits and of the Forests* and various backpacking magazines. Her novels include *The Long Trail, Yellowthroat, Montana Feathers* and *Grassy Flats.* She is presently working on her fifth book, entitled *Kathleen O'Donald.*

PHYLLIS HORN, like the characters in her short story, lived in cotton-mill-owned housing throughout her childhood. A native of North Carolina, she now lives in Virginia with her partner of fifteen years. Author of *The Chesapeake Project* and *Lodestar,* Phyllis's third novel is called *North Beach.*

MARY J. JONES lives on the seacoast of Iowa. Author of *Avalon* (1991) and — coming soon — *Harpquest.*

KARIN KALLMAKER was born in 1960 and raised by loving, middle-class parents in Sacramento, California. From an average childhood and equally unremarkable public school adolescence, she went on to obtain an ordinary bachelor's degree from the California State University at Sacramento. Sometime between junior high and college — age sixteen, to be exact — she fell into the arms of her first and only sweetheart. It seemed like a perfectly normal thing to do. In 1985, she and her sweetheart saw the film *Desert Hearts.* The end credit stating, "based on the book by Jane Rule" led to a rewarding search at the Berkeley Public Library through a section in the card catalog labeled "Lesbianism—Fiction." Karin credits her lover's tenacity in wading through title after title to find self-affirming books by and about lesbians as the encouragement she needed to forget about the so-called mainstream and write her first romance for lesbians. That manuscript became her first Naiad Press book, *In Every Port.* Now a full-time financial manager in the nonprofit sector, she lives in Oakland with that same sweetheart; she is a one-woman woman.

Karin is also the editor of *Uncommon Voices,* the bi-monthly publication of the Bay Area Career Women, which is the largest lesbian social organization in the United States. In addition to *In*

Every Port, she has authored the best-selling *Touchwood* and *Paperback Romance.* Her fourth Naiad romance will be *Car Pool.* Since Karin considers her lesbian readers to be the only mainstream, she intends to write many more.

LEE LYNCH has published nine books with Naiad Press: *Toothpick House, Old Dyke Tales, The Swashbuckler, Home in Your Hands, Dusty's Queen of Hearts Diner, The Amazon Trail, Sue Slate — Private Eye, That Old Studebaker* and *Morton River Valley.* Her new short story collection, *Cactus Love,* will be published by Naiad in 1993. Her syndicated column, "The Amazon Trail," appears in over a dozen papers in the U.S. and Canada. She is active in environmental issues and in fighting the powerful conservative movement that is attacking our rights to publish, print, sell or buy lesbian literature.

VICKI P. McCONNELL hails from Hays, Kansas, but has lived in Oklahoma City, Denver, Los Angeles, and currently resides in Seattle. A senior editor for two trade magazines, she also created the first illustrated lesbian mystery series featuring reporter Nyla Wade in Naiad Press titles *Mrs. Porter's Letter* (1982), *Burnton Widows* (1984) and *Double Daughter* (1988). Naiad also published McConnell's first novel, *Berrigan,* in 1978, with a new edition including author afterword in 1990.

McConnell is forty-three, single, a Libra, and her license plate reads WORD-UP. Her checkered journalistic past includes ghosting the autobiography of an oil baroness/crook, self-publishing "erotica politica" poetry (*Sense You* — 1979), profiling Mapplethorpe model and body builder Lisa Lyon, and suggesting the good vibrations possible with sex toys for *Colorado Woman News*. She is also a freelance writer for *The Advocate* (including articles on PWA writers' groups and gay themes in television) and *Square Pegs* (coverage of the Lambda Awards and the article "Does Incest Make You Gay?"). Following a recent trend, she is working on a novel featuring her pet as a main character. She also proudly confounds fashion police and gender wardens with frequent use of her own personal *International Male* credit card.

ISABEL MILLER is the author of *Patience and Sarah, The Love of Good Women, Side by Side,* and *A Dooryard Full of Flowers.* She lives tenderly in upstate New York.

ELISABETH NONAS was born in New York City in 1949. She moved to Los Angeles in 1977, where she wrote her first two novels, *For Keeps* (1985) and *A Room Full of Women* (1990), both published by Naiad Press. *A Room Full of Women* has been optioned and is being made into a motion picture.

Elisabeth teaches fiction writing at UCLA Extension, and developed and taught the first lesbian and gay fiction writing classes offered there.

She has written scripts for television, as well as articles for *The Advocate*. She recently completed a screenplay based on Paul Monette's novel *Afterlife* for Triangle Productions. She is currently working on her third novel for Naiad, *Staying Home*.

ROBBI SOMMERS resides in northern California. She is the author of the bestselling lesbian erotica *Pleasures, Players, Kiss and Tell* and *Uncertain Companions*. Currently thigh-high in research for her soon-to-be-released book, *Behind Closed Doors*, she often asks herself, "Is it hot in here or is it me?"

DOROTHY TELL is fifty-three, proud mother and grandmother by chance, grateful monogamous lesbian (twenty years by choice. She and Ruth, her lover/writing partner/daily inspiration/ and light-of-her-post-menopausal-life, cohabit with their good friend and cherished companion, Gladys. In a beautiful home on a blue Texas lake they strive to make manifest their dream of "croneworks."

Dot loves to fish, but has almost no time for it. She writes from three to six a.m. and drives 600 miles each week as she slogs through the thousand remaining days until she can retire from the "job from hell" and write full-time.

Her works include *Wilderness Trek* (romance, 1990), *Murder at Red Rook Ranch* (first Poppy Dillworth mystery, 1990), *The Hallelujah Murders* (second Poppy Dillworth mystery, 1991), and coming soon, *The Goddess Murders* (third Poppy Dillworth mystery).

SHIRLEY VEREL was born in London, and lives there ... English lecturer. Gazette columnist. Left-wing feminist. Agnostic. Has dachshund called Hester. Published a number of books of which two novels, *The Other Side of Venus,* and *The Bee's Kiss,* are published by Naiad Press.

AMANDA KYLE WILLIAMS and her partner of six years live just outside Atlanta, Georgia with their ever-growing family of cats.

Amanda Kyle Williams is the best-selling author of *Club Twelve,* the first espionage thriller to feature a lesbian agent, the Lambda Literary Award-nominated *Providence File,* and *A Singular Spy.* Her fourth Madison McGuire espionage thriller, *The Spy in Question* will be available in 1993.

MOLLEEN ZANGER is a forty-four-year-old Michigan Dyke who is finally in her fourth (but not final) year of college. She lives in a small town with her mate, youngest son, three dogs, two cats and assorted cacti. Her first novel, *The Year Seven,* is scheduled for release by Naiad in 1993.

LOOKING FOR NAIAD?

Buy our books at
www.naiadpress.com

or call our toll-free number
1-800-533-1973

or by fax (24 hours a day)
1-850-539-9731

DEATH UNDERSTOOD by Claire McNab. 240 pp. 2nd Denise Cleever
thriller.   ISBN 1-56280-264-X $11.95

TREASURED PAST by Linda Hill. 208 pp. A shared passion for
antiques leads to love.   ISBN 1-56280-263-1 $11.95

UNDER SUSPICION by Claire McNab. 224 pp. 12th Detective
Inspector Carol Ashton mystery.   ISBN 1-56280-261-5 $11.95

UNFORGETTABLE by Karin Kallmaker. 288 pp. Can each
woman win her true love's heart?   ISBN 1-56280-260-7   11.95

MURDER UNDERCOVER by Claire McNab. 192 pp. 1st Denise
Cleever thriller.   ISBN 1-56280-259-3   11.95

EVERYTIME WE SAY GOODBYE by Jaye Maiman. 272 pp.
7th Robin Miller mystery.   ISBN 1-56280-248-8   11.95

SEVENTH HEAVEN by Kate Calloway. 240 pp. 7th Cassidy
James mystery.   ISBN 1-56280-262-3   11.95

STRANGERS IN THE NIGHT by Barbara Johnson. 208 pp. Her
body and soul react to a stranger's touch. ISBN 1-56280-256-9   11.95

THE VERY THOUGHT OF YOU edited by Barbara Grier and
Christine Cassidy. 288 pp. Erotic love stories by Naiad Press
authors.   ISBN 1-56280-250-X   14.95

TO HAVE AND TO HOLD by PeGGy J. Herring. 192 pp. Their
friendship grows to intense passion . . .   ISBN 1-56280-251-8   11.95

INTIMATE STRANGER by Laura DeHart Young. 192 pp.
Ignoring Tray's myserious past, could Cole be playing with fire?
                                            ISBN 1-56280-249-6   11.95

SHATTERED ILLUSIONS by Kaye Davis. 256 pp. 4th
Maris Middleton mystery.   ISBN 1-56280-252-6   11.95

SET UP by Claire McNab. 224 pp. 11th Detective Inspector Carol
Ashton mystery.   ISBN 1-56280-255-0   11.95

THE DAWNING by Laura Adams. 224 pp. What if you had the power to change the past? ISBN 1-56280-246-1   11.95

NEVER ENDING by Marianne K. Martin. 224 pp. Temptation appears in the form of an old friend and lover. ISBN 1-56280-247-X   11.95

ONE OF OUR OWN by Diane Salvatore. 240 pp. Carly Matson has a secret. So does Lela Johns. ISBN 1-56280-243-7   11.95

DOUBLE TAKEOUT by Tracey Richardson. 176 pp. 3rd Stevie Houston mystery. ISBN 1-56280-244-5   11.95

CAPTIVE HEART by Frankie J. Jones. 176 pp. Love in the fast lane or heartside romance? ISBN 1-56280-258-5   11.95

WICKED GOOD TIME by Diana Tremain Braund. 224 pp. In charge at work, out of control in her heart. ISBN 1-56280-241-0   11.95

SNAKE EYES by Pat Welch. 256 pp. 7th Helen Black mystery. ISBN 1-56280-242-9   11.95

CHANGE OF HEART by Linda Hill. 176 pp. High fashion and love in a glamorous world. ISBN 1-56280-238-0   11.95

UNSTRUNG HEART by Robbi Sommers. 176 pp. Putting life in order again. ISBN 1-56280-239-9   11.95

BIRDS OF A FEATHER by Jackie Calhoun. 240 pp. Life begins with love. ISBN 1-56280-240-2   11.95

THE DRIVE by Trisha Todd. 176 pp. The star of *Claire of the Moon* tells all! ISBN 1-56280-237-2   11.95

BOTH SIDES by Saxon Bennett. 240 pp. A community of women falling in and out of love. ISBN 1-56280-236-4   11.95

WATERMARK by Karin Kallmaker. 256 pp. One burning question . . . how to lead her back to love? ISBN 1-56280-235-6   11.95

THE OTHER WOMAN by Ann O'Leary. 240 pp. Her roguish way draws women like a magnet. ISBN 1-56280-234-8   11.95

SILVER THREADS by Lyn Denison.208 pp. Finding her way back to love . . . ISBN 1-56280-231-3   11.95

CHIMNEY ROCK BLUES by Janet McClellan. 224 pp. 4th Tru North mystery. ISBN 1-56280-233-X   11.95

OMAHA'S BELL by Penny Hayes. 208 pp. Orphaned Keeley Delaney woos the lovely Prudence Morris. ISBN 1-56280-232-1   11.95

SIXTH SENSE by Kate Calloway. 224 pp. 6th Cassidy James mystery. ISBN 1-56280-228-3   11.95

DAWN OF THE DANCE by Marianne K. Martin. 224 pp. A dance with an old friend, nothing more . . . yeah! ISBN 1-56280-229-1   11.95

THOSE WHO WAIT by Peggy J. Herring. 160 pp. Two sisters . . . in love with the same woman. ISBN 1-56280-223-2   11.95

WHISPERS IN THE WIND by Frankie J. Jones. 192 pp. "If you don't want this," she whispered, "all you have to say is 'stop.'"
ISBN 1-56280-226-7   11.95

WHEN SOME BODY DISAPPEARS by Therese Szymanski. 192 pp. 3rd Brett Higgins mystery.   ISBN 1-56280-227-5   11.95

UNTIL THE END by Kaye Davis. 256pp. 3rd Maris Middleton mystery.   ISBN 1-56280-222-4   11.95

FIFTH WHEEL by Kate Calloway. 224 pp. 5th Cassidy James mystery.   ISBN 1-56280-218-6   11.95

JUST YESTERDAY by Linda Hill. 176 pp. Reliving all the passion of yesterday.   ISBN 1-56280-219-4   11.95

THE TOUCH OF YOUR HAND edited by Barbara Grier and Christine Cassidy. 304 pp. Erotic love stories by Naiad Press authors.   ISBN 1-56280-220-8   14.95

WINDROW GARDEN by Janet McClellan. 192 pp. They discover a passion they never dreamed possible.   ISBN 1-56280-216-X   11.95

PAST DUE by Claire McNab. 224 pp. 10th Carol Ashton mystery.   ISBN 1-56280-217-8   11.95

CHRISTABEL by Laura Adams. 224 pp. Two captive hearts and the passion that will set them free.   ISBN 1-56280-214-3   11.95

PRIVATE PASSIONS by Laura DeHart Young. 192 pp. An unforgettable new portrait of lesbian love . . .   ISBN 1-56280-215-1   11.95

BAD MOON RISING by Barbara Johnson. 208 pp. 2nd Colleen Fitzgerald mystery.   ISBN 1-56280-211-9   11.95

RIVER QUAY by Janet McClellan. 208 pp. 3rd Tru North mystery.   ISBN 1-56280-212-7   11.95

ENDLESS LOVE by Lisa Shapiro. 272 pp. To believe, once again, that love can be forever.   ISBN 1-56280-213-5   11.95

FALLEN FROM GRACE by Pat Welch. 256 pp. 6th Helen Black mystery.   ISBN 1-56280-209-7   11.95

THE NAKED EYE by Catherine Ennis. 208 pp. Her lover in the camera's eye . . .   ISBN 1-56280-210-0   11.95

OVER THE LINE by Tracey Richardson. 176 pp. 2nd Stevie Houston mystery.   ISBN 1-56280-202-X   11.95

LOVE IN THE BALANCE by Marianne K. Martin. 256 pp. Weighing the costs of love . . .   ISBN 1-56280-199-6   11.95

PIECE OF MY HEART by Julia Watts. 208 pp. All the stuff that dreams are made of —   ISBN 1-56280-206-2   11.95

MAKING UP FOR LOST TIME by Karin Kallmaker. 240 pp. Nobody does it better . . .   ISBN 1-56280-196-1   11.95

GOLD FEVER by Lyn Denison. 224 pp. By author of *Dream Lover*.   ISBN 1-56280-201-1   11.95

WHEN THE DEAD SPEAK by Therese Szymanski. 224 pp. 2nd
Brett Higgins mystery.   ISBN 1-56280-198-8   11.95

FOURTH DOWN by Kate Calloway. 240 pp. 4th Cassidy James
mystery.   ISBN 1-56280-193-7   11.95

CITY LIGHTS COUNTRY CANDLES by Penny Hayes. 208 pp.
About the women she has known . . .   ISBN 1-56280-195-3   11.95

POSSESSIONS by Kaye Davis. 240 pp. 2nd Maris Middleton
mystery.   ISBN 1-56280-192-9   11.95

A QUESTION OF LOVE by Saxon Bennett. 208 pp. Every
woman is granted one great love.   ISBN 1-56280-205-4   11.95

RHYTHM TIDE by Frankie J. Jones. 160 pp.   . . . to desire
passionately and be passionately desired.   ISBN 1-56280-189-9   11.95

PENN VALLEY PHOENIX by Janet McClellan. 208 pp. 2nd
Tru North Mystery.   ISBN 1-56280-200-3   11.95

OLD BLACK MAGIC by Jaye Maiman. 272 pp. 6th Robin
Miller mystery.   ISBN 1-56280-175-9   11.95

LEGACY OF LOVE by Marianne K. Martin. 240 pp. Women
will do anything for her . . .   ISBN 1-56280-184-8   11.95

LETTING GO by Ann O'Leary. 160 pp. Laura, at 39, in love
with 23-year-old Kate.   ISBN 1-56280-183-X   11.95

LADY BE GOOD edited by Barbara Grier and Christine Cassidy.
288 pp. Erotic stories by Naiad Press authors.   ISBN 1-56280-180-5   14.95

CHAIN LETTER by Claire McNab. 288 pp. 9th Carol Ashton
mystery.   ISBN 1-56280-181-3   11.95

NIGHT VISION by Laura Adams. 256 pp. Erotic fantasy romance
by "famous" author.   ISBN 1-56280-182-1   11.95

SEA TO SHINING SEA by Lisa Shapiro. 256 pp. Unable to resist
the raging passion . . .   ISBN 1-56280-177-5   11.95

THIRD DEGREE by Kate Calloway. 224 pp. 3rd Cassidy James
mystery.   ISBN 1-56280-185-6   11.95

WHEN THE DANCING STOPS by Therese Szymanski. 272 pp.
1st Brett Higgins mystery.   ISBN 1-56280-186-4   11.95

PHASES OF THE MOON by Julia Watts. 192 pp. . . . . hungry
for everything life has to offer.   ISBN 1-56280-176-7   11.95

BABY IT'S COLD by Jaye Maiman. 256 pp. 5th Robin Miller
mystery.   ISBN 1-56280-156-2   10.95

CLASS REUNION by Linda Hill. 176 pp. The girl from her
past . . .   ISBN 1-56280-178-3   11.95

DREAM LOVER by Lyn Denison. 224 pp. A soft, sensuous,
romantic fantasy.   ISBN 1-56280-173-2   11.95

FORTY LOVE by Diana Simmonds. 288 pp. Joyous, heart-
warming romance.   ISBN 1-56280-171-6   11.95

IN THE MOOD by Robbi Sommers. 160 pp. The queen of
erotic tension! ISBN 1-56280-172-4 11.95

SWIMMING CAT COVE by Lauren Wright Douglas. 192 pp. 2nd
Allison O'Neil Mystery. ISBN 1-56280-168-6 11.95

THE LOVING LESBIAN by Claire McNab and Sharon Gedan.
240 pp. Explore the experiences that make lesbian love unique.
ISBN 1-56280-169-4 14.95

COURTED by Celia Cohen. 160 pp. Sparkling romantic
encounter. ISBN 1-56280-166-X 11.95

SEASONS OF THE HEART by Jackie Calhoun. 240 pp. Romance
through the years. ISBN 1-56280-167-8 11.95

K. C. BOMBER by Janet McClellan. 208 pp. 1st Tru North
mystery. ISBN 1-56280-157-0 11.95

LAST RITES by Tracey Richardson. 192 pp. 1st Stevie Houston
mystery. ISBN 1-56280-164-3 11.95

EMBRACE IN MOTION by Karin Kallmaker. 256 pp. A whirlwind
love affair. ISBN 1-56280-165-1 11.95

HOT CHECK by Peggy J. Herring. 192 pp. Will workaholic Alice
fall for guitarist Ricky? ISBN 1-56280-163-5 11.95

OLD TIES by Saxon Bennett. 176 pp. Can Cleo surrender to a
passionate new love? ISBN 1-56280-159-7 11.95

COSTA BRAVA by Marta Balletbo-Coll. 144 pp. Read the book,
see the movie! ISBN 1-56280-160-0 11.95

MEETING MAGDALENE & OTHER STORIES by
Marilyn Freeman. 144 pp. Read the book, see the movie!
ISBN 1-56280-170-8 11.95

SECOND FIDDLE by Kate Kalloway. 208 pp. 2nd P.I. Cassidy James
mystery. ISBN 1-56280-161-9 11.95

LAUREL by Isabel Miller. 128 pp. By the author of the beloved
Patience and Sarah. ISBN 1-56280-146-5 10.95

LOVE OR MONEY by Jackie Calhoun. 240 pp. The romance of
real life. ISBN 1-56280-147-3 10.95

SMOKE AND MIRRORS by Pat Welch. 224 pp. 5th Helen Black
Mystery. ISBN 1-56280-143-0 10.95

DANCING IN THE DARK edited by Barbara Grier & Christine
Cassidy. 272 pp. Erotic love stories by Naiad Press authors.
ISBN 1-56280-144-9 14.95

TIME AND TIME AGAIN by Catherine Ennis. 176 pp. Passionate
love affair. ISBN 1-56280-145-7 10.95

PAXTON COURT by Diane Salvatore. 256 pp. Erotic and wickedly
funny contemporary tale about the business of learning to live
together. ISBN 1-56280-114-7 10.95

INNER CIRCLE by Claire McNab. 208 pp. 8th Carol Ashton
Mystery.   ISBN 1-56280-135-X   11.95

LESBIAN SEX: AN ORAL HISTORY by Susan Johnson.
240 pp. Need we say more?   ISBN 1-56280-142-2   14.95

WILD THINGS by Karin Kallmaker. 240 pp. By the undisputed
mistress of lesbian romance.   ISBN 1-56280-139-2   11.95

NOW AND THEN by Penny Hayes. 240 pp. Romance on the
westward journey.   ISBN 1-56280-121-X   11.95

DEATH AT LAVENDER BAY by Lauren Wright Douglas. 208 pp.
1st Allison O'Neil Mystery.   ISBN 1-56280-085-X   11.95

YES I SAID YES I WILL by Judith McDaniel. 272 pp. Hot
romance by famous author.   ISBN 1-56280-138-4   11.95

FORBIDDEN FIRES by Margaret C. Anderson. Edited by Mathilda
Hills. 176 pp. Famous author's "unpublished" Lesbian romance.
                                       ISBN 1-56280-123-6   21.95

SIDE TRACKS by Teresa Stores. 160 pp. Gender-bending
Lesbians on the road.   ISBN 1-56280-122-8   10.95

WILDWOOD FLOWERS by Julia Watts. 208 pp. Hilarious and
heart-warming tale of true love.   ISBN 1-56280-127-9   10.95

NEVER SAY NEVER by Linda Hill. 224 pp. Rule #1: Never get
involved with . . .   ISBN 1-56280-126-0   11.95

THE WISH LIST by Saxon Bennett. 192 pp. Romance through
the years.   ISBN 1-56280-125-2   10.95

OUT OF THE NIGHT by Kris Bruyer. 192 pp. Spine-tingling
thriller.   ISBN 1-56280-120-1   10.95

FAMILY SECRETS by Laura DeHart Young. 208 pp. Enthralling
romance and suspense.   ISBN 1-56280-119-8   10.95

INLAND PASSAGE by Jane Rule. 288 pp. Tales exploring conven-
tional & unconventional relationships. ISBN 0-930044-56-8   10.95

DOUBLE BLUFF by Claire McNab. 208 pp. 7th Carol Ashton
Mystery.   ISBN 1-56280-096-5   11.95

BAR GIRLS by Lauran Hoffman. 176 pp. See the movie, read
the book!   ISBN 1-56280-115-5   10.95

THE FIRST TIME EVER edited by Barbara Grier & Christine
Cassidy. 272 pp. Love stories by Naiad Press authors.
                                       ISBN 1-56280-086-8   14.95

MISS PETTIBONE AND MISS McGRAW by Brenda Weathers.
208 pp. A charming ghostly love story. ISBN 1-56280-151-1   10.95

CHANGES by Jackie Calhoun. 208 pp. Involved romance and
relationships.   ISBN 1-56280-083-3   10.95

FAIR PLAY by Rose Beecham. 256 pp. An Amanda Valentine
Mystery.   ISBN 1-56280-081-7   10.95

PAYBACK by Celia Cohen. 176 pp. A gripping thriller of romance, revenge and betrayal. ISBN 1-56280-084-1   10.95

THE BEACH AFFAIR by Barbara Johnson. 224 pp. Sizzling summer romance/mystery/intrigue. ISBN 1-56280-090-6   10.95

GETTING THERE by Robbi Sommers. 192 pp. Nobody does it like Robbi! ISBN 1-56280-099-X   10.95

FINAL CUT by Lisa Haddock. 208 pp. 2nd Carmen Ramirez Mystery. ISBN 1-56280-088-4   10.95

FLASHPOINT by Katherine V. Forrest. 256 pp. A Lesbian blockbuster! ISBN 1-56280-079-5   10.95

CLAIRE OF THE MOON by Nicole Conn. Audio Book — Read by Marianne Hyatt. ISBN 1-56280-113-9   13.95

FOR LOVE AND FOR LIFE: INTIMATE PORTRAITS OF LESBIAN COUPLES by Susan Johnson. 224 pp. ISBN 1-56280-091-4   14.95

DEVOTION by Mindy Kaplan. 192 pp. See the movie — read the book! ISBN 1-56280-093-0   10.95

SOMEONE TO WATCH by Jaye Maiman. 272 pp. 4th Robin Miller Mystery. ISBN 1-56280-095-7   10.95

GREENER THAN GRASS by Jennifer Fulton. 208 pp. A young woman — a stranger in her bed. ISBN 1-56280-092-2   10.95

TRAVELS WITH DIANA HUNTER by Regine Sands. Erotic lesbian romp. Audio Book (2 cassettes) ISBN 1-56280-107-4   13.95

CABIN FEVER by Carol Schmidt. 256 pp. Sizzling suspense and passion. ISBN 1-56280-089-1   10.95

THERE WILL BE NO GOODBYES by Laura DeHart Young. 192 pp. Romantic love, strength, and friendship. ISBN 1-56280-103-1   10.95

FAULTLINE by Sheila Ortiz Taylor. 144 pp. Joyous comic lesbian novel. ISBN 1-56280-108-2   9.95

OPEN HOUSE by Pat Welch. 176 pp. 4th Helen Black Mystery. ISBN 1-56280-102-3   10.95

ONCE MORE WITH FEELING by Peggy J. Herring. 240 pp. Lighthearted, loving romantic adventure. ISBN 1-56280-089-2   11.95

WHISPERS by Kris Bruyer. 176 pp. Romantic ghost story. ISBN 1-56280-082-5   10.95

PAINTED MOON by Karin Kallmaker. 224 pp. Delicious Kallmaker romance. ISBN 1-56280-075-2   11.95

THE MYSTERIOUS NAIAD edited by Katherine V. Forrest & Barbara Grier. 320 pp. Love stories by Naiad Press authors. ISBN 1-56280-074-4   14.95

DAUGHTERS OF A CORAL DAWN by Katherine V. Forrest. 240 pp. Tenth Anniversay Edition. ISBN 1-56280-104-X   11.95

BODY GUARD by Claire McNab. 208 pp. 6th Carol Ashton
Mystery.   ISBN 1-56280-073-6   11.95

SECOND GUESS by Rose Beecham. 216 pp. An Amanda
Valentine Mystery.   ISBN 1-56280-069-8   9.95

A RAGE OF MAIDENS by Lauren Wright Douglas. 240 pp.
6th Caitlin Reece Mystery.   ISBN 1-56280-068-X   10.95

TRIPLE EXPOSURE by Jackie Calhoun. 224 pp. Romantic
drama involving many characters.   ISBN 1-56280-067-1   10.95

PERSONAL ADS by Robbi Sommers. 176 pp. Sizzling short
stories.   ISBN 1-56280-059-0   11.95

CROSSWORDS by Penny Sumner. 256 pp. 2nd Victoria Cross
Mystery.   ISBN 1-56280-064-7   9.95

SWEET CHERRY WINE by Carol Schmidt. 224 pp. A novel of
suspense.   ISBN 1-56280-063-9   9.95

CERTAIN SMILES by Dorothy Tell. 160 pp. Erotic short stories.
                                            ISBN 1-56280-066-3   9.95

EDITED OUT by Lisa Haddock. 224 pp. 1st Carmen Ramirez
Mystery.   ISBN 1-56280-077-9   9.95

SMOKEY O by Celia Cohen. 176 pp. Relationships on the
playing field.   ISBN 1-56280-057-4   9.95

KATHLEEN O'DONALD by Penny Hayes. 256 pp. Rose and
Kathleen find each other and employment in 1909 NYC.
                                            ISBN 1-56280-070-1   9.95

STAYING HOME by Elisabeth Nonas. 256 pp. Molly and Alix
want a baby . . . or do they?   ISBN 1-56280-076-0   10.95

TRUE LOVE by Jennifer Fulton. 240 pp. Six lesbians searching
for love in all the "right" places.   ISBN 1-56280-035-3   11.95

THE ROMANTIC NAIAD edited by Katherine V. Forrest &
Barbara Grier. 336 pp. Love stories by Naiad Press authors.
                                            ISBN 1-56280-054-X   14.95

UNDER MY SKIN by Jaye Maiman. 336 pp. 3rd Robin Miller
Mystery.   ISBN 1-56280-049-3.   11.95

CAR POOL by Karin Kallmaker. 272pp. Lesbians on wheels
and then some!   ISBN 1-56280-048-5   11.95

NOT TELLING MOTHER: STORIES FROM A LIFE by Diane
Salvatore. 176 pp. Her 3rd novel.   ISBN 1-56280-044-2   9.95

GOBLIN MARKET by Lauren Wright Douglas. 240pp. 5th Caitlin
Reece Mystery.   ISBN 1-56280-047-7   10.95

BEHIND CLOSED DOORS by Robbi Sommers. 192 pp. Hot,
erotic short stories.   ISBN 1-56280-039-6   11.95

CLAIRE OF THE MOON by Nicole Conn. 192 pp. See the
movie — read the book!   ISBN 1-56280-038-8   11.95

SILENT HEART by Claire McNab. 192 pp. Exotic Lesbian
romance.   ISBN 1-56280-036-1   11.95

SAVING GRACE by Jennifer Fulton. 240 pp. Adventure and
romantic entanglement.   ISBN 1-56280-051-5   11.95

CURIOUS WINE by Katherine V. Forrest. 176 pp. Tenth Anniver-
sary Edition. The most popular contemporary Lesbian love story.
                                            ISBN 1-56280-053-1   11.95
    Audio Book (2 cassettes)   ISBN 1-56280-105-8   13.95

A PROPER BURIAL by Pat Welch. 192 pp. 3rd Helen Black
Mystery.   ISBN 1-56280-033-7   9.95

LOVE, ZENA BETH by Diane Salvatore. 224 pp. The most talked
about lesbian novel of the nineties!   ISBN 1-56280-030-2   10.95

A DOORYARD FULL OF FLOWERS by Isabel Miller. 160 pp.
Stories incl. 2 sequels to *Patience and Sarah.*   ISBN 1-56280-029-9   9.95

MURDER BY TRADITION by Katherine V. Forrest. 288 pp. 4th
Kate Delafield Mystery.   ISBN 1-56280-002-7   11.95

THE EROTIC NAIAD edited by Katherine V. Forrest & Barbara
Grier. 224 pp. Love stories by Naiad Press authors.
                                            ISBN 1-56280-026-4   14.95

DEAD CERTAIN by Claire McNab. 224 pp. 5th Carol Ashton
Mystery.   ISBN 1-56280-027-2   11.95

CRAZY FOR LOVING by Jaye Maiman. 320 pp. 2nd Robin Miller
Mystery.   ISBN 1-56280-025-6   11.95

UNCERTAIN COMPANIONS by Robbi Sommers. 204 pp.
Steamy, erotic novel.   ISBN 1-56280-017-5   11.95

A TIGER'S HEART by Lauren Wright Douglas. 240 pp. 4th Caitlin
Reece Mystery.   ISBN 1-56280-018-3   9.95

PAPERBACK ROMANCE by Karin Kallmaker. 256 pp. A
delicious romance.   ISBN 1-56280-019-1   11.95

THE LAVENDER HOUSE MURDER by Nikki Baker. 224 pp.
2nd Virginia Kelly Mystery.   ISBN 1-56280-012-4   9.95

PASSION BAY by Jennifer Fulton. 224 pp. Passionate romance,
virgin beaches, tropical skies.   ISBN 1-56280-028-0   11.95

STICKS AND STONES by Jackie Calhoun. Contemporary
lesbian lives and loves.
Audio Book (2 cassettes)   ISBN 1-56280-106-6   13.95

UNDER THE SOUTHERN CROSS by Claire McNab. 192 pp.
Romantic nights Down Under.   ISBN 1-56280-011-6   11.95

GRASSY FLATS by Penny Hayes. 256 pp. Lesbian romance in
the '30s.   ISBN 1-56280-010-8   9.95

KISS AND TELL by Robbi Sommers. 192 pp. Scorching stories
by the author of *Pleasures.*   ISBN 1-56280-005-1   11.95

IN THE GAME by Nikki Baker. 192 pp. 1st Virginia Kelly
Mystery.   ISBN 1-56280-004-3   9.95

STRANDED by Camarin Grae. 320 pp. Entertaining, riveting
adventure.   ISBN 0-941483-99-1   9.95

THE DAUGHTERS OF ARTEMIS by Lauren Wright Douglas.
240 pp. 3rd Caitlin Reece Mystery.   ISBN 0-941483-95-9   9.95

THE HALLELUJAH MURDERS by Dorothy Tell. 176 pp. 2nd
Poppy Dillworth Mystery.   ISBN 0-941483-88-6   8.95

BENEDICTION by Diane Salvatore. 272 pp. Striking, contemporary romantic novel.   ISBN 0-941483-90-8   11.95

TOUCHWOOD by Karin Kallmaker. 240 pp. Loving, May/
December romance.   ISBN 0-941483-76-2   11.95

COP OUT by Claire McNab. 208 pp. 4th Carol Ashton Mystery.
                                            ISBN 0-941483-84-3   10.95

THE BEVERLY MALIBU by Katherine V. Forrest. 288 pp. 3rd
Kate Delafield Mystery.   ISBN 0-941483-48-7   11.95

THE PRICE OF SALT by Patricia Highsmith (writing as Claire
Morgan). 288 pp. Classic lesbian novel, first issued in 1952 . . .
acknowledged by its author under her own, very famous, name.
                                            ISBN 1-56280-003-5   12.95

SIDE BY SIDE by Isabel Miller. 256 pp. From beloved author of
Patience and Sarah.   ISBN 0-941483-77-0   9.95

STAYING POWER: LONG TERM LESBIAN COUPLES by
Susan E. Johnson. 352 pp. Joys of coupledom. ISBN 0-941483-75-4   14.95

SLICK by Camarin Grae. 304 pp. Exotic, erotic adventure.
                                            ISBN 0-941483-74-6   9.95

NINTH LIFE by Lauren Wright Douglas. 256 pp. 2nd Caitlin
Reece Mystery.   ISBN 0-941483-50-9   9.95

MURDER AT RED ROOK RANCH by Dorothy Tell. 224 pp.
1st Poppy Dillworth Mystery.   ISBN 0-941483-80-0   8.95

THEME FOR DIVERSE INSTRUMENTS by Jane Rule. 208 pp.
Powerful romantic lesbian stories.   ISBN 0-941483-63-0   8.95

DEATH DOWN UNDER by Claire McNab. 240 pp. 3rd Carol
Ashton Mystery.   ISBN 0-941483-39-8   11.95

THERE'S SOMETHING I'VE BEEN MEANING TO TELL YOU
Ed. by Loralee MacPike. 288 pp. Gay men and lesbians coming out
to their children.   ISBN 0-941483-44-4   9.95

LIFTING BELLY by Gertrude Stein. Ed. by Rebecca Mark. 104 pp.
Erotic poetry.   ISBN 0-941483-51-7   10.95

AFTER THE FIRE by Jane Rule. 256 pp. Warm, human novel by
this incomparable author.   ISBN 0-941483-45-2   8.95

PLEASURES by Robbi Sommers. 204 pp. Unprecedented
eroticism.   ISBN 0-941483-49-5   11.95

EDGEWISE by Camarin Grae. 372 pp. Spellbinding
adventure.   ISBN 0-941483-19-3   9.95

FATAL REUNION by Claire McNab. 224 pp. 2nd Carol Ashton
Mystery.   ISBN 0-941483-40-1   11.95

IN EVERY PORT by Karin Kallmaker. 228 pp. Jessica's sexy,
adventuresome travels.   ISBN 0-941483-34-7   11.95

OF LOVE AND GLORY by Evelyn Kennedy. 192 pp. Exciting
WWII romance.   ISBN 0-941483-32-0   10.95

CLICKING STONES by Nancy Tyler Glenn. 288 pp. Love
transcending time.   ISBN 0-941483-31-2   9.95

SOUTH OF THE LINE by Catherine Ennis. 216 pp. Civil War
adventure.   ISBN 0-941483-29-0   8.95

WOMAN PLUS WOMAN by Dolores Klaich. 300 pp. Supurb
Lesbian overview.   ISBN 0-941483-28-2   9.95

THE FINER GRAIN by Denise Ohio. 216 pp. Brilliant young
college lesbian novel.   ISBN 0-941483-11-8   8.95

LESSONS IN MURDER by Claire McNab. 216 pp. 1st Carol Ashton
Mystery.   ISBN 0-941483-14-2   11.95

YELLOWTHROAT by Penny Hayes. 240 pp. Margarita, bandit,
kidnaps Julia.   ISBN 0-941483-10-X   8.95

SAPPHISTRY: THE BOOK OF LESBIAN SEXUALITY by
Pat Califia. 3d edition, revised. 208 pp.   ISBN 0-941483-24-X   12.95

THE SECRET IN THE BIRD by Camarin Grae. 312 pp. Striking,
psychological suspense novel.   ISBN 0-941483-05-3   8.95

TO THE LIGHTNING by Catherine Ennis. 208 pp. Romantic
Lesbian 'Robinson Crusoe adventure. ISBN 0-941483-06-1   8.95

DREAMS AND SWORDS by Katherine V. Forrest. 192 pp.
Romantic, erotic, imaginative stories. ISBN 0-941483-03-7   11.95

MEMORY BOARD by Jane Rule. 336 pp. Memorable novel
about an aging Lesbian couple.   ISBN 0-941483-02-9   12.95

THE ALWAYS ANONYMOUS BEAST by Lauren Wright Douglas.
224 pp. 1st Caitlin Reece Mystery. ISBN 0-941483-04-5   8.95

These are just a few of the many Naiad Press titles — we are the oldest and
largest lesbian/feminist publishing company in the world. We also offer an
enormous selection of lesbian video products. Please request a complete
catalog. We offer personal service; we encourage and welcome direct mail
orders from individuals who have limited access to bookstores carrying our
publications.